THIS BOOK
BELONGS TO

VINTAGE CLASSICS

# Mark Svendsen

# TO DIE FOR

## VINTAGE CLASSICS

Australia

A Vintage Classic Children's book
Published by Random House Australia Pty Ltd
Level 3, 100 Pacific Highway, North Sydney NSW 2060
www.randomhouse.com.au

First published by Woolshed Press in 2011
This Vintage Classic Children's edition published in 2012

Addresses for companies within the Random House Group can be found at
www.randomhouse.com.au/offices.

National Library of Australia
Cataloguing-in-Publication Entry

Author: Svendsen, Mark
Title: To die for / Mark Svendsen
Edition: 2nd ed.
ISBN: 978 1 74275 745 2 (pbk.)
Target Audience: For primary school age
Subjects: Adventure stories
Dewey Number: A823.3

Cover illustration by Tony Flowers
Cover design by Astred Hicks, www.designcherry.com
Dory illustration by Ben Redlich
Internal design and typesetting by Midland Typesetters, Australia
Printed in Australia by Griffin Press, an accredited ISO AS/NZS 14001:2004
Environmental Management System printer

Random House Australia uses papers that are natural, renewable and
recyclable products and made from wood grown in sustainable forests.
The logging and manufacturing processes are expected to conform to the
environmental regulations of the country of origin.

For my father
Nestor Svendsen
(1927–2008)

*where love has been*
*grace remains forever*

*See the back of the book*
*for a labelled diagram of a dory*

Young Fisherwoman:
Call back the men who have gone to
cast their nets ...
These are not times for men to dare the sea,
When moon and wind and water plot
against them.

Old Fisherwoman:
Be still, young wife. Giant mackerel sweep
the coast, ...
Hear this from one who lost her son at sea ...
Hold down your fear, and drown it in
your heart.

Val Vallis (1916–2009)
from 'Fishing Season' in
*Songs of the East Coast*

# CHAPTER 1

A movement of shadows, cut through by honey-light from the kerosene lantern, woke him on his fourteenth birthday just as it did every night before the first grey of morning. His father breathed onto the kindling in the wood stove in the kitchen to coax the fire into flame. He was making himself coffee before he fried the remains of yesterday's bread with sardines for breakfast.

That crackle of flame, the sizzling smell of sardines, the tunk of the metal firebox door, the snapping of kindling had been the song of his mornings longer than Christos could remember. It was the song of a fisherman preparing for the sea. His father's leaving song.

It was always dark when he left the house with the spoon-lures Christos or one of his younger brothers had sharpened and polished the evening before. The spoons, a meal for mid-morning and a small bait net were all packed into a sugar bag that had a piece of old rope sewn to the bottom and tied tight around the top to form a shoulder strap. A twenty-litre drum of diesel and his torch and his father was ready for the day's fishing.

His father would take this load and stow it in the boat, then take the empty bag up the Esplanade for ice from the iceworks, all before the night began to fade. A professional fisherman had to be fishing the reef in the first grey of dawn, before the blue took its place in the sky. To fish any later was not worth getting up for.

Most days Christos would lie in bed, his sea-blue eyes half-closed, listening, watching and drifting. He'd swim with her through sweet dreams, diving beneath her and swimming all around, splashing her with laughter and water. He could tell, as is the way in dreams, without seeing, that she was happy to be with him. She ducked down beneath the surface. He lost sight of her for a moment before she resurfaced face to face, laughing before him.

'Do you want to kiss me?' she giggled.

*Do I ever!*

Her body floated close to his. He closed his eyes and puckered his lips for her mermaid's kiss. He waited a long, tantalising moment before … she laughed and was gone, splashing his sad, puppy-dog face with a spray of water.

He always woke up then, frustrated with the memory of what he'd been dreaming. Once, just a week ago, his father had put his head in through the curtained doorway and smiled awkwardly when he saw Christos's face.

'Not so long back you didn't want to know girls,' his father said, as though he too had seen the dream. 'Things are changing, boy.'

But there was no sleeping in this morning – this morning Christos was going fishing too. Often before he had prepared himself alongside his father, during the school holidays and on weekends. But this morning would be the first time he was allowed to take the small dory out by himself.

*I'll take her out and stay out for the night, if I haven't caught too many fish that is!*

Today was his birthday present and he intended to enjoy it all by himself. It wasn't that he didn't like other people, it was just that he always felt happiest when he was alone with the sea, the boat, the sky.

*It's always good at sea, and if I manage to catch enough fish to fill the icebox I'll come home straight-away, because then everyone will be happy here too.*

'He's too young,' his mother said, wrinkles of care furrowing the corners of her eyes. 'If the wind blows up he doesn't have the strength. It's a man's game. He's still a boy.'

He couldn't remember his mother ever being

out of bed at this time of the morning before. She was wrapped in a worn dressing-gown.

*She looks beautiful with her hair unbrushed.*

'The wind won't blow up,' his father answered. 'And even if it does, Christos knows where to anchor to sit out the blow. We've done it before.'

His mother looked doubtful, her eyes narrowing as she stared at his father.

'Nothing will happen, woman,' he reassured her gently, placing his hand on her shoulder.

'Well ...' she murmured. Unconvinced, she glanced at Christos. 'Couldn't you just go out with your father?' Christos shook his head defiantly.

*And you won't let me take anyone with me either, will you?* He thought it, but said nothing. *I could lose the whole trip here and now if I don't play my cards right.* He pretended to be tired, rubbing the sleep from his eyes and shifting his weight impatiently from foot to foot. One of his sisters half-uttered a word as she rolled over in bed. It sounded as if she was agreeing with his mum.

*Thanks for nothing!* Christos thought angrily, but he managed to keep his face calm as a lapping sea.

Finally, with a half-sigh of resignation, his mother asked, 'Well, are you ready to go then?'

Christos nodded firmly and that was that.

Christos knew, at least he thought he knew, he could do it. His father always said, 'You'll never know if you don't have a go.'

*If Dad says I'm ready I'm at least going to have a fair crack at it. Besides, Dad's always right, isn't he?*

His mother didn't interfere with his father's preparations, but her eyes followed his movements carefully, watching as he filled two sugar bags, putting a sleeping bag and a second water bottle in Christos's. Then they drank their mugs of hot tea, ate their fried bread with sardines, the garlic brown and sweet, and were finally ready to leave.

Christos knew his father resented his mother's presence and he knew she was holding herself back from coming into the kitchen to cook breakfast for them both. She couldn't resist completely. When his father went back into the bedroom for his leather-covered watch, his mother grabbed an extra half-loaf of bread and put it in Christos's bag. She saw him looking at her.

'In case you stay the night,' she explained.

'I'll eat the fish I catch,' Christos answered. *Do you think I'm going out just for fun, Mum?* His mother nodded, agreeing about eating fish, but patted the bag closed with a look on her face that said, '*It never hurts to be sure.*' She pushed his fringe out of his eyes.

When his father returned Christos stood to leave, torch in hand. His mother stepped towards him then, pulling her son close. She was warm and soft in her old dressing-gown and Christos blushed as she kissed him on both his cheeks.

'Happy birthday,' she said and then, standing back, slipped a gold medallion on a chain over his head and tucked it inside his shirt. She placed her hand over it.

'I dreamed about you last night, Chris,' she said. 'On your first trip.' Her look seemed somehow sad. It sounded as though she hadn't finished. Christos waited to hear more but his father drew a deep breath and turned to go.

'Happy birthday,' his mother repeated. 'Be careful.'

He touched her arm before he followed his father out into the night.

His father leaned down to pick up his drum of fuel from the verandah before they padded barefoot down the creaking back stairs, out the back gate and into the alley. Then they went down through the sleeping town. Coils of grey fog kissed Christos's face, as soft as his mother's new-washed hair.

*It's the second day of fog. That means more tomorrow. Fantastic! When the fog lifts it'll be calm and the sea oily and flat as a mirror. And if I stay overnight it'll still be perfect for coming home. Imagine the scene. Everybody will be there when I arrive with the icebox and the kill-pit both overflowing with fish!* He smiled at the thought.

Christos turned to wave but his mother had closed the verandah door, blocking out all light.

The darkness was huge. Even the streetlight at the next corner was invisible. He switched on his torch but it was embarrassingly bright. His mother had insisted on a new battery. He turned it off again, choosing to follow close behind his father and his torch beam. They walked on, passing other open kitchen doors that cast uneven oblongs of light into the street before the fog swallowed them too and the night shrank about the fishermen once more. As they approached the wharf others joined their ranks, silent but for their barefoot steps, and all with their small torches hardly yellowing the ground before their feet, like a Milky Way of muffled stars flowing down to the sea.

*Is she ever awake in the mornings like I am?* Christos wondered. Her father worked in the meatworks. He too was up before the light.

*Maybe in the mornings she lies half-awake just like me. So what does she think about? Does she dream what I dream? Does it fill her with light and air and happiness? Do I tease her, in her dream, splashing her face with water? Do I ask her if she wants a kiss?*

Christos jostled down onto the wharf behind his father, shifting the weight of the bag. The extra gear made it heavier and it cut into his thin shoulder.

*Mothers!*

They stepped down from the wharf onto the *Tradewinds*'s deck. His father's boat was much bigger than the dory and not so sleek, but still their weight rocked her where she rode. Crossing the deck, Christos leaned down to place his bag in the dory's kill-pit. He was happy to be rid of the weight, rubbing his shoulders, stretching and wiping his long fringe from his eyes. The air felt warm and cool at the same time like it did on foggy mornings. The smell of salt was so strong it was nearly a taste.

*She would know about the taste of the fog, just like me. Did her father ever take her fishing?* He knew that her family went out to the islands to camp sometimes in the holidays. She told the other girls and he heard about it from them.

*I bet she's good at fishing. All it takes is knowing*

*how to think like a fish! She's good at that, thinking like other people. Like in the school musical. Acting's just pretending to be someone else. How hard can it be to pretend to be a fish?*

The *Tradewinds* knocked gently against the dory, nudging him from his daydream. The dory was too small to have an official name, but in his own mind Christos always called her *Li'l Bit*. His father's boat was more than three times as long and proudly bore the name *Tradewinds* on her transom and both sides of her bow. His father had painted the letters in fastidious black print outlined in gold. The other fishermen laughed, saying that the name looked like a solicitor's business card. One even said quietly, 'Or an undertaker's', and regretted immediately that he had. *Li'l Bit* was Christos's name alone, not written for anyone else to see.

'Stow the gear.' His father spoke barely above a whisper, as though his voice might break the morning's silent spell. He put the fuel and gear in the kill-pit and slung the empty bag back onto his shoulder. 'I'll get your ice.'

Christos nodded. He could almost hear his father's sermon on keeping things shipshape. *'Everything in its place and a place for everything, Chris. There's no mistakes that way.'* Christos slapped his arms around his body trying to get the blood flowing.

*Have to wake up properly or I'll forget something and be in strife.*

He began on the *Tradewinds*, stowing his father's food, fuel, net and lures before climbing down onto *Li'l Bit*'s fog-wet foredeck. He pulled off the hatch cover, lowering his bag down next to the anchor, away from the kill-pit and the motor where his food might get spoiled, then walked back across the slippery deck, placing his feet down carefully for balance like a heron fishing in the shallows. He stepped over the stowed outrigger as *Li'l Bit* rocked like a cradle.

Christos took off the hatch to the standing-pit, sat on the coaming and slid his legs in until his feet were firm on the plywood floor. He placed the torch in the line tray behind him and then put the spoons into the basket under the deck with the pliers, lines, knives, the spare trace wire, donger, gloves and all the other gear. Finally he stowed the hatch cover and untied the tiller, his bare foot snaking out until it touched the cold metal arm.

*Now everything's in place and there's only Dad and the ice to wait for.* Pushing the tiller to and fro, he felt the weight of the water resisting it, rocking *Li'l Bit* slightly from side to side.

*Where is the old man? I should be out there now, not hanging around here waiting! I wonder if she'd come fishing with me if I asked her? What would her mother say? Maybe we could just sneak out together? Does she even like going fishing?* The question stumped him.

*I always thought she did. Why? Because I do? No, because I want her to like it! Not the best reason I suppose. Maybe she thinks it's cruel. Some of the other girls do.* But he thought it was no crueller to kill a mackerel than it was to kill a bullock like her father did.

*Li'l Bit* dipped violently as his father swung on board and lowered the ice into the kill-pit.

Christos opened the lid of the icebox, slid the heavy block of ice into it, pulled the lid shut and handed the bag back to his father. He could hear motors coughing into life all over the harbour.

*Better hurry if I want to be first out on my birthday.*

'Get her warmed up,' his father said. Christos nodded and opened the hinged hatch. He leaned in and switched the fuel on, set the throttle, checked the motor was out of gear, lifted the decompression lever, took the crank-handle from its cradle and fitted it to the shaft.

His father's eyes seemed to burn into his back, measuring his every action, assessing how well he did everything that was required.

*Haven't you got anything else to do, old man?*

He turned the handle slowly through most of one revolution until he felt the slight resistance of the compression.

*I've started this motor a hundred times before so why doesn't he put the ice bag away or something, anything other than standing there watching me.*

Christos put one hand on the decompression

lever and pushed down hard on the handle, pulling it through once, twice, three times, then dropped the valve. But the motor coughed hard, kicking back on the handle and jarring his arm.

'Damn!' he snapped. Red shame began to burn on his neck.

*At least I can get my hand out of the way without it getting caught!* He remembered the times his father got his big hands belted by the handle when *Li'l Bit* kicked back. The memory made him feel better.

'Here, Squirt,' his father said, asking for a turn, but Christos was determined not to fail the first test of the day.

*Stop calling me that! How'd you like it if I called you Beer-barrel or Keg or something? I can't help being small for my age.*

'I'd better be able to do it myself!' Christos growled. 'You won't be there to help me later.'

His father raised his eyebrows, nodded, and shrugged slightly. 'Fair enough,' he agreed. He leaned back against *Tradewinds* and crossed his arms to wait.

Christos lifted the valve and repeated the process.

*First feel for the compression, then wind through once and, on the second stroke this time, drop the valve.* The motor fired, revving far too fast. He adjusted the throttle and closed the lid, quietening the noise. It sounded like thunder in the fog where all close sound was amplified. The exhaust left a black smudge of oil where it spluttered out halfway up the side of the hull.

Christos smiled to himself as he pulled on the bow line that secured *Li'l Bit* to the *Tradewinds*.

*Two turns is what Dad always takes to start the motor when it's cold. Two strokes is what I just did. No problem!*

*Li'l Bit's* bow separated from *Tradewinds*, heading seaward. Only the stern line held her now. His father jumped back onto *Tradewinds* as the gap between the vessels widened.

'Hold your horses, Chris! I'm not off yet! Where'll ya go?' his father continued urgently, as though feeling he needed to offer advice now because he wouldn't be able to later.

'Hummocky,' Christos answered. He could see the lights on some of the closer boats beginning to move. He pushed hard against the tiller.

'Too far,' his father said as he untied the stern line. He knew it would be well after fishing time when the boy arrived. Christos glanced at his father with a determined look, pulling the line in as he did.

'Your choice, of course!' His father answered the challenge in his son's eyes. 'Fish the shoals on the way out. You never know your luck,' he suggested, without insisting. 'Here, I brought you some fresh gar.'

Christos took the baitfish his father offered and laid them in the line tray.

*I'll put them away later. It's time to go.* He pushed off and *Li'l Bit* floated free.

His father stood with the ice bag hanging empty in his hand. 'Don't do anything stupid,' he called, rubbing his fingers through his hair, knowing he sounded like a nag. 'Watch out for the Noahs!'

Christos shook his head almost apologetically at his father.

*As if I can't deal with sharks. What's he take me for?* He pushed the gear lever forward with his foot. The motor took the strain and the prop spun slowly, swirling like a big fish darting off from just under the surface, disturbing the face of the water.

At last he was going, going out to the islands where the blue sea slept under its grey blanket of fog. To where he'd put his lines down into the deep. To where he'd be free, himself – Christos, the fisherman!

*Mum wouldn't worry if she could see me now. If only Karis was here.* Christos turned the tiller to bear away from the *Tradewinds.* His present had begun.

# CHAPTER 2

Christos listened for sounds in the fog as he steered *Li'l Bit* out of the harbour. Other motors idled but he could hear none was underway. He revved *Li'l Bit* until she was well over the four-knot harbour speed limit.

*Too bad. Try and catch me now!* The wet surfaces of the rocks reflected his torch's light as he steered as close to them as he could. Hugging the harbour wall would get him out there fishing faster. All the boats were supposed to show running lights, but most of the smaller craft just shone their torches from their decks.

'Only a bloody idiot'd ram someone,' the fishermen said. 'And he'd deserve what he had coming if he did.'

*Wonder what Dad would do if I rammed* Li'l Bit *into someone or hit the harbour wall?* He'd seen the backhander his father gave a deckhand on the *Tradewinds* once. It was a smack, a thud of flesh, that almost knocked the younger man over the side. All because he hadn't closed the icebox lid properly and the ice had begun to melt.

*But I won't do anything stupid, will I, so it won't happen to me.*

Christos watched the fog more closely then, listening to the water sluice between the rocks and feeling the waves' faint slap against *Li'l Bit's* hull, reading the sea's signs in the darkness. Even though it was always calm under the fog there was still a change in the luff of breeze and the lilt of broken waves as they cleared the harbour wall. Christos turned to look.

*No lights near me. I'm first out!* He smiled and

brought *Li'l Bit* around to bear east, checking his bearing on the compass under the front lip of the standing-pit. Due east for five minutes, then south-east. *Li'l Bit* surged onward into the darkness as he kicked the throttle lever hard forward with his foot. He judged from the revving of the motor that she was making about five knots – just a notch off flat out.

Christos sat back and made himself comfortable. He squinted at the phosphorescent points on the hands of his watch.

*Four a.m. It'll be an hour and a bit before I hit the first shoal off the end of Divided. Of course Dad's right. I won't make it to Hummocky to fish by first light, but if there's nothing biting at Divided I'll push on and make it there for the change of tide later in the morning. Probably won't catch anything that late, but today's supposed to be my birthday present. Who cares about fishing anyway! Until then there's nothing to do but sit back and relax. I'll slow Li'l Bit down in about seventy-five minutes and listen to where I am. Maybe I should check the lines again?*

The motor hummed. *Li'l Bit* slapped her bow into the long broaching swells.

Christos wondered whether his mother had stayed awake after they'd left. He would never say so to anybody but it was nice to think she was worried about him. He folded his arms across his chest.

*Don't worry, Mum, I'll be fine.*

Cold water ran down his neck as he motored southwards through the fog. He reached around to turn up his collar and caught the chain his mother had given him in his fingers. He pulled the medallion from beneath his shirt and leaned down to the torchlight. It was oval and quite heavy. One side was flat and golden. He turned it over in his hand. The other side bore the image of a cross embossed with the figure of a man dressed in robes. On his back the man carried a child. Christos looked closer. Underneath the figure were some words he could just make out: *Saint Christopher Protect Us.*

*It's my name — well, almost. Saint Christos,*

*patron saint of fishing trips*. His face broke into a wide grin.

*Thanks, Mum.* He switched off the torch and slipped the medallion back under his shirt where it lay cold against his skin.

Christos slapped his hands for warmth and checked his watch again. Only five minutes since last time.

*I want to be there now, catching fish, not sitting here waiting!* He frowned to himself. 'Half-cocked Chris' was what his father called him.

*Which is worse than calling me Squirt. I can't help being the smallest kid in my class or getting excited about things.* The name was all because of what happened on his first proper fishing trip.

*We were on Tradewinds, me and Dad and Grandad, when I was about ten years old. I've always known Dad wanted me to be a fisherman. He always says that salt water runs in my veins. My great-grandfather was a fisherman, so were my grandad and Dad. Now it's my turn.*

'Get the lines out,' Dad ordered over his shoulder as he steered Tradewinds into position along the edge of a school of baitfish. Grandad nodded to me. I ducked down under the transom and pulled out three reels. I remember I was almost vibrating with excitement, like the amplifier attached to an electric guitar sounds when it's first turned on. I was buzzing with energy. I grabbed my line and started feeding it out over the stern. I was down past the sinkers when something made me turn around. Dad was staring at me, his mouth half-open in disbelief, trying not to laugh aloud.

'Forgotten something, mate?' he asked. I felt like someone just pulled the plug out of my stomach and my guts slipped out. No bait! On his first proper trip Christos the fisherman threw in his line with no bait! Dad roared with laughter.

'Just steer the boat,' Grandad growled at Dad, though he was smiling too as he turned to me. 'And you pull that line back in.' Once I'd retrieved my line Grandad swapped it for a gar-baited one. 'Now show us what you're made of, son,' he said. So I did. My first fish was twelve kilos. It almost killed me to land it, and then Dad made me dong it dead, to 'finish the job'.

'Not bad,' my father said. I still remember Grandad picking up the fish, pulling the hooks out from the corner of its mouth, wiping some of its blood onto the point of my nose.

'Now you're a fisherman,' he said.

But I'm not sure I want to be a fisherman. I love fishing. No, that isn't quite right. I love the sea and fishing's a great way to be out at sea.

And what about Karis? What does she think about it? What would I do if she wanted me at home for a party on the weekend, not out at the Swains waiting a week on the reef for the weather to change so I could get back in? Maybe I could slaughter cattle like her father does instead? It wouldn't be so bad, would it? Nothing could be bad if we were together every night. Christos settled back to enjoy the thought, content, for now, to wait.

After an hour he could nearly make out the shape of the long swell. In some patches it was almost clear near the surface, with the tattered fog wafting above it like a torn curtain blowing in a white breeze. He whistled through his bottom teeth as he played a game to pass the time, rocking *Li'l Bit* to port so the exhaust puttered and splotted into the side of the swells. He checked the compass as the fog paled to a slightly lighter grey. Impatiently he checked his watch one last time.

*Divided must be close by now.*

Christos pushed back on the throttle until the motor idled quietly, then kicked the gear lever into neutral, letting *Li'l Bit* glide. The following wake caught up with the dory and slapped against her stern, urging her forward. He strained forward too, trying to catch the sound of waves on rocks. But the sea was rising and falling silently without enough force to splinter the swell against the shore.

*There'll only be the suck of the water as it washes through the rock channels. It's almost impossible to hear unless I'm really close. Damn the fog!*

'Hoy!' he shouted between funnelled hands, short and sharp towards where he expected the island to be. He waited for an echo. But there was no sound, at least nothing he could hear above the blubbering of the exhaust. Unless it was a hiss of what sounded like air.

*What was that?* Christos crawled forward and killed the motor, waiting for it to die into silence before he called out again. This time he heard nothing, his voice deadened by the blanket of fog.

*Maybe I imagined it? Should be close. Can't be sure.* The fog coiled tight around him, hemming him in. He began to feel uncertain.

*What if I misjudged my speed on the way out? If I went too fast maybe I've missed Divided? I can usually feel where the breeze is stopped by the island, and the movement of the waves changes behind it. But not today, not the first time I'm alone. No, of course not! No breeze, no waves. Maybe Mum was right? Maybe I am too young?* Christos called out loudly again, his voice cracking with the effort. Nothing. He tried to think of another way to tell where he was.

*I need to make a sound that'll travel.* They used bells on ships, he knew, but he didn't have a bell.

*Something metal maybe?* Christos thought quickly. *What have I got? The anchor!* He jumped out of the kill-pit, clambering towards the for'ard hatch where the anchor was stowed.

*Anyway, if the worst comes to the worst I can just wait until the fog lifts.* He opened the hatch, but as he bent to climb in, *Li'l Bit* jolted upwards, rolling violently to port. Christos lost his footing and fell facedown, hitting the hatch coaming just above his eye.

The bow of the dory lifted clear of the water and she pitched more viciously than before. His legs and hips slipped off the edge. Only his torso remained on board. He was slipping off into the dark water below. Christos threw himself back towards the boat, kicking down with his feet, clawing for a hold. His foot hit something, something hard that gave under his weight.

*Shark!*

Shark filled his mind. He kicked down hard off its back. Grabbing hold of the lip of the hatch, he threw himself back on board, flopping like a fish out of water. Beneath him a huge darkness filled the ocean. With his weight suddenly thrust across to the other side of the deck, the dory broached to starboard as suddenly as it had earlier to port. Now Christos was slipping off the other side. Quickly he slid towards the stern, rolling into the safety of the kill-pit, his heart hammering like a frightened child at the door of a locked room.

But then a mist, warmer than the surrounding fog, rained down on him. He laughed aloud as he lay on his back in the kill-pit waiting for his heart to slow.

*That explains the hissing sound. You idiot!* He crawled to the edge, hung his head over and gazed in awe at the leviathan gliding only an arm's length under the surface.

The humpback had been lounging like a lump on the skin of the sea. When the dory bumped into it, it simply took the opportunity to scratch its back against *Li'l Bit*'s keel. Christos knew the dory could take the rubbing without any danger. As he watched, the whale moved beyond the boat, gliding effortlessly with the current.

He'd seen whales before, often, but he'd never been so close.

*It's beautiful. Magnificent, that's the word I'm looking for. An immense gliding lump, heaving the huge tons of its body onwards with the force of an ocean swell.* The whale reminded him of Tiny Hudson, the biggest man he knew. His hands could completely encircle Christos's head like a motorcycle helmet. They said his fists could crush a man's chest with one blow. But Tiny Hudson was always gentle because if he held anything too tight, or forced it too hard, it would shatter in his hands. The whale could smash *Li'l Bit* into a thousand pieces but it knew its massive power and held itself back, disciplined itself to be gentle, not to hurt any blameless smaller thing.

Christos shook his head as he sat upright in the kill-pit.

*What would Dad say if he saw me now? He'd be choking with laughter, just like he did at my first rugby game. I remember catching the ball, but when I looked down the field I saw this huge, fat* kid barrelling in to tackle me. I just did what any sensible little eight-year-old would do – threw the ball straight up in the air!

'I surrender!' Dad yelled from the sideline, and he laughed and laughed.

There are some things, Chris, that the old man doesn't need to know. It would have been dangerous if I'd fallen overboard, but . . . I didn't and that's the end of that. It would have been a different story if I'd hit it at full speed though. But I didn't do that either. The whale can be my little secret. I'll always remember it but I don't have to tell anyone . . . ever. Well, maybe I could tell her, when I trust her enough not to go blabbing off to the other girls. Why do they do that, girls? Mum says my sisters gossip like fishmongers' wives. She always laughs when she says it though, because she's a fisherman's wife herself.

I must have missed the island and be to the seaward of Divided. Whales rarely come to the leeward side. That's why I didn't hear an echo when I yelled, because the island's somewhere behind me, not in front. If I go further to sea in this fog I might miss Hummocky as well and end up in New Zealand! I have to find Divided first and go from there.

Christos couldn't rely on his watch to tell him how long he should travel, or in which direction, not if he wasn't certain from what point he was starting.

*It'd be different if I could see something. The fog should be gone by nine a.m., but sometimes it doesn't lift until eleven or later. Too long not to know where in the South Pacific I am! Besides the sun's almost up. I should be out there slaying 'em. I don't have enough fuel to be motoring round forever. I need to find Divided now.*

Christos stood up, took a deep breath of salty fog air, wiped his face and opened the hatch to restart the motor.

# CHAPTER 3

It was his lucky day. Once he'd turned the dory around and yelled a few more times, Christos heard an echo from the rocky cliffs. The sun was just clear of the horizon, he guessed, so he hadn't missed too much fishing time. It was easy now there was more light. It wasn't bright in the fog but there was enough sunlight for the spoons to glitter when he finally got them fishing. He motored past Divided, backtracking so he could fish the shoal that led into the island from the western side.

Christos kicked *Li'l Bit* out of gear and let her drift while he worked. Taking two reels from the standing-pit he climbed into the kill-pit and unlashed the outrigger pole. As he slid it into its brackets the outrigger rocked up and down like a paintbrush painting a wall. Christos stepped back down into the standing-pit, taking out the gloves and pulling them on. He clapped his hands together to try to get some feeling so he could handle the lines, before he kicked the dory into action.

Setting the throttle at about four and a half knots, he steered *Li'l Bit* into position close to the edge of the shoal. The lines would fish as near to the reef as possible.

'Right on the sweet spot,' his father would say. 'Dead on the money.'

Christos fed out the short outrigger line first. The transom line followed, long and heavy-leaded, to fish deep behind the turbulence of the dory's wake. Finally he secured both the lines to their cleats and stowed the reels.

*Come and get it, fishies!* The lines seemed to

stretch and recoil on their rubber shock absorbers. If there was a strike on either line the shockie would stretch like an elastic band before it sprang back, jabbing the hook into the fish's mouth. Well, that was the theory. Christos preferred to hold the transom line in his hand, ready to jerk back hard to set the hook if a fish struck. He'd seen too many lost on the shockies. But they were still handy to keep the tension on one line if you were lucky enough to have a fish on both lines at once.

Christos stood side-on in the kill-pit, half-watching the way ahead and half the lines behind. He pulled the transom line in a bit and wrapped it twice around his hand, ready to work it backwards and forwards like a hunted baitfish trying to escape.

'Calling them in,' his father called it. Enticing, like a girl's perfume at the movies.

Suddenly *Li'l Bit* skewed to starboard.

*Strike!* A fish bit at the silver spoon at the end of the outrigger line.

*It's going to be a good morning!* Christos dropped the transom line and grabbed the cord to the outrigger. He steered *Li'l Bit* in a wide arc to circle around the fish and shorten the distance he had to pull. He could feel its weight as it fought like a dog struggling to be free of a chain. For a moment it made him think.

*What must it feel like to have a hook piercing your mouth, sharp as a knife, that drags you, fighting, to your fate?*

But the mackerel shook him from his thoughts. It ran, arcing away from the dory, yanking Christos's arm hard. He wasn't holding the line properly and it flicked from his grasp back out onto the outrigger shockie.

'Damn!' Christos swore without thinking, just as his father did if something went wrong. He reached out again but did it properly this time, hitting the line from underneath with the top side of his hand, then quickly throwing two wraps around his palm.

*Wrap it around your fingers by mistake and a big fish'll rip them off!* This wasn't a big fish, but it wasn't little either. It felt like a snook – eight kilos maybe. He dragged on the cord, hand over hand, laying it into the transom tray. Soon he was down to the wire. It was thin and sharp even through the gloves. His arms began to feel the strain.

The fish threw its head from side to side before it ran again. But this time he was ready. The tight line sliced through the sea swell, cutting the water's surface like a kite string slicing sky. There was enough sun now to see the water droplets beading the straining wire, pinging off when the fish shuddered in the depths. Christos hauled on the line, wrapped it, and dragged again. The fish went deep and cut back dangerously close to the propeller. He leaned over the side and held the line as far away from the prop as he could. The fish obliged and ran to starboard again.

*Dad catches fish this size one after another when they're biting. He sweats and grunts, but his arms are strong. My arms are starting to ache with just one fish.*

*Are you a sook or something, Chris? Have a go!* Only ten metres of trace left. The fish was tiring fast too, its zigzags more desperate the shorter the line grew. Christos prepared himself for the last effort. He could see the mackerel swimming beside the dory. He took a deep breath.

*Timing's everything now. One more long reach down the trace, two wraps and it's – into the kill-pit.* He could hear his father's voice sweet-talking the fish, 'Come in out of the wet, darling. You'll catch your death!'

Christos threw his weight backwards, twisting his body like a dancer. In one clean arc he swung the fish clear of the water, over the gunwale and into the kill-pit.

The fish lay there snapping its broken-needle teeth, gasping in the air-world, shuddering and fighting, flipping and flicking still. Christos grabbed the donger and waited a moment for a clear shot before he brought it down on the back of the fish's head with a dull, wooden thud. He had to hit it quickly again, before it shuddered and died. And again he heard his father's words.

'*Kill it quick, for Christ's sake! No one wants to die slow.*'

The fish lay still, rainbows glistening on its skin. It shone like opal in the dull light and, for a moment, Christos felt a pang for its dead beauty. He grabbed the pliers and yanked the hook from its mouth as the transom line jerked hard on the shockie.

*No rest for the wicked. Get amongst 'em, Chris! They're striking like snakes!*

He grabbed the second line. This fish felt smaller. *Probably a doggie. Lucky 'cause I'm already tired.* He let the transom line go and lowered the outrigger spoon back into the water, lifting his hands above his head to avoid tangles as he paid out the line.

*Li'l Bit* had circled completely while he'd caught his first fish. Christos steered the boat back along the reef. He'd bring the fish to port, to avoid fouling the outrigger line. He grabbed the transom line and hauled it in quickly. Again and again he pulled, his arms beginning to quiver with the strain. The extra leads that made it swim deep meant it was much heavier than the outrigger line, even without a fish, and it was much longer too.

The fish ran in an arc from side to side across the wake of the dory. Water dripped from Christos's face, hot sweat mixed with fog. The fish was more desperate now, zigzagging quicker as the line shortened.

*It's not the size of the dog in the fight, but the size of the fight in the doggie! Down to the trace. Twenty metres to go.* The leads were in the transom tray. The line was lighter now but his back ached. His arms began to shake uncontrollably, like a mountain climber who's used all his strength. He was bent double over the line tray and panting as if he'd run a race. He needed to rest but there was no choice except to go on. Hand over hand. Or maybe lose the fish. His arms shook. He stopped, panting. He held but couldn't win any line.

*Can't do it. I need to breathe!*

Christos double-wrapped, straining to hold on with both hands like a sailor to a mainsail sheet in a storm.

*Only ten metres but the fish might as well be in Fiji.* He felt like he was pulling the plug out of the bottom of the sea.

*Maybe Mum's right, maybe I need the strength of a man. Where'll I get that? Buy it at the Fishermen's Co-op?* He tried to smile.

'You'll never know if you don't have a go,' his father said inside his head. 'Put some back into it, son.'

*You'd do it if Karis was here!*

Christos took three deep breaths then pulled hard and fast, shaking the line free from his gloves quickly as he reefed the armfuls in.

The line sliced the sea's skin like a razor blade. He could almost hear it buzz, vibrating like a violin string. But then the fish was there, beside the dory.

*Bigger than I thought, maybe ten kilos. Not a tiddler, but not huge either. Still, don't be nice till it's on the ice!* Christos knew he hadn't caught it yet. He bent down, wrapped the line, then leaned back, trying to throw the fish into the kill-pit. But he was tired. His timing was out. The fish hit the gunwale, teetering on the edge. Christos lunged forward to try and grab the line as the fish flipped to escape – straight into the kill-pit. How lucky was that? He tried to laugh but was panting too much. He grabbed the donger and hit the fish hard on the head – once, twice, then a third time to be sure, because he felt as weak as a kitten and didn't trust his arm to have enough strength to kill a thing.

Replacing the donger with a quivering hand, Christos breathed deeply, his heart thumping.

*Almost stuffed it ... but not quite!* As he sucked in his breath he tried to decide. *I've got a couple of fish so maybe I should just head out to Hummocky.* He could hear his father's voice, *'Keep fishing. They're biting like savage dogs.'*

*I've already got nearly enough to pay for the fuel and that's before this arvo and tomorrow morning.* Christos laughed aloud. He was already winding in the trace on the transom line.

*Apparently I've decided!* He pulled in the line quickly and stowed the reel. Then he looked up.

The jagged black teeth of the reef leered from the mist ten metres in front of him, jutting from the sea. Christos threw the tiller full to port. *Li'l Bit* slewed to starboard. The rocks were so close he could smell them. He held his breath, closed his eyes.

*What an idiot! Watch where you're going!* He felt the swell catch the dory, lifting it in towards the rocks. Closer. Closer. He opened his eyes. He was so close he could almost reach out and touch the oysters. Then the swell fell away from under them and *Li'l Bit* slipped down. It was a miracle they hadn't hit anything. Just as he dared to breathe again, the retreating wave pulled the dory downward and the next swell threatened to swamp them from behind. *Li'l Bit* strained away, the motor groaning as they were sucked downward. For a moment they seemed to sit still, poised between rocks and wave, until, as though she had been released by an invisible hand, *Li'l Bit* lifted up and they were underway again, steaming out of danger. Christos loved his little dory then.

*You'll never let me down, will you? You're my best friend. Well, after my mates at school, and Karis, if I ever get up the courage to actually talk to her.*

But Christos felt cold.

*That's the second time today I've almost come to grief.* He squatted down in the standing-pit. He could almost feel the back of his father's hand belting him across the ear.

*'Stuff it up once and you've learnt something. Stuff it up twice, you're a bloody idiot!'* But he recovered quickly. *Dad'll never know. I'll never tell him, and besides this is my birthday, mine, mine, mine and my boat to command.*

'We're a great team, you and me,' Christos said, patting *Li'l Bit*'s deck. He steered back to follow the reef before crossing it in a safe depth of water and heading out to the open sea.

*I should stay while the fish are biting.* Christos glanced into the kill-pit. *But I have those two already. That's enough even if I don't get any more.* Christos leaned forward and opened the throttle as far as he could. *Li'l Bit* surged to meet the swell. Under his shirt his new medallion tapped his chest.

It's an omen. Two bad things have happened but third time counts for all. Christos smiled broadly, his mind was already on Hummocky. Third time lucky.

# CHAPTER 4

A slight breeze wafted across the surface of the ocean, lifting the bottom of the white fog like his mother's hand fluffing his feather quilt. His father always said the sea only becomes the ocean when you can't see the land. Christos frowned a little.

*I can't see land until I almost run into it!* A slow smile crept across his face. He couldn't stay worried for too long. After all, nothing bad had actually happened and nothing was hurt, except his pride.

*Now just admit what you really want to do. You really want to sleep the night on Hummocky after you've explored. Then you can fish the evening tide till the icebox is full and fill up the kill-pit in the morning. That's a real plan!*

Christos flattened down his unruly hair with both hands. A bead of water trickled down his neck. He swiped at it like it was a mosquito.

*When the fog lifts it'll be a perfect September day. Blue sky, blue sea, flat as oil. The islands will stand out so clearly, it'll seem as though they've dragged their anchors and moved closer to the shore during the night.*

Christos wished that she was here. He wished they'd shared the fog, getting lost, the whale, the fish, the rocks, the whole adventure.

*It needn't be her really,* he told himself, *it might just as easily be Mum and Dad or my brothers and sisters, mates from school. I just prefer the idea of it being her. Why wouldn't I?*

If it was his family who were there with him the trip would become a story for telling on rainy days.

'Remember the time we ran into the whale?' his sister would ask as a tropical low drenched the country outside with stinging, wind-whipped rain.

'It was my birthday,' he'd reply. His younger brothers would stop playing whatever game they were into to listen. Then they'd share their story, each with their slightly different version. Each remembering different details.

'It was ...'

'And then ...'

'Remember ...?'

*But it's too hard to remember a whole story yourself, your head isn't big enough. My story is just one little piece of thousands of other people's stories and I'm part of thousands of their stories too.*

Christos thought about the idea. It made him feel like a tiny speck on the vast face of the ocean. Insignificant, but part of the huge story that was the sea.

*But nobody's here except me so I'll have to try to remember everything – the smell of the sea, the touch of fog, how annoying it is when it dribbles inside your shirt, the sound of the swell as it rises and falls against the rocks, the glisten of light on the fish's skin, the red of their blood on the kill-pit deck, the rock-black tons of the breathing whale. I can feel my head getting bigger just thinking about it!*

Christos laughed. But thinking about blood on the kill-pit deck reminded him there was still work to be done.

*It's too dangerous to clean the fish while I'm steaming, too easy for the knife to slip. I'll do it when I get there. In the meantime they need to be on ice.* Christos tied the tiller in place, clambering into the kill-pit to lift the lid of the icebox and slip the fish inside.

As he stood there the fog seemed to tear open and for a moment he was drenched by sunlight, strong on his face, the sea and sky turquoise around him and above. Rolls of long, broad swells moved across the sea's surface passing through that magic space. Christos felt as if he had been flying through clouds and suddenly burst from the side of one, like the god of all creation. He turned to face *Li'l Bit*'s bow, standing still in the kill-pit with his legs braced apart.

Then he lifted his arms to fly, the breeze in his face, the sun on his hair. He closed his eyes, dazzled by the feeling, opening his mouth to let the air in, gulping it down like cold water, drinking in the spring morning. He leaned slowly to starboard, arms still outstretched, eyes closed. *Li'l Bit* leaned with him, like they were surfing on a slow, never-ending wave, thrumming across the sea. Then he leaned slowly to port and *Li'l Bit* heeled back, tilting under his weight as he felt the long swell lift them up, raising them like wind under an osprey's wings.

*I remember the first time I met her, when she was the new girl at school. She spoke to me. 'My name's Karis. What's yours?'*

*I just stood there staring. I'd never seen anybody so ... beautiful before. I remember feeling my mouth open but I didn't say a thing. Nothing at all. I was too full of ... I felt like I do right now.*

*She could have laughed at me, but she didn't. She said, 'Are you okay?'*

*When I didn't answer she still didn't laugh, she just turned away with that look on her face that meant she wanted to know more about me before she'd make up her mind about just how crazy I was.*

Christos felt his heart pump in his chest. Heard the breath empty from his lungs, heard them fill again. But then his stomach interrupted, rumbling matter-of-factly, and then the fog closed again, swallowing the sun. Christos opened his eyes, blinking as though he'd just woken up.

'I'll remember this day,' he said to *Li'l Bit*. 'I'll remember because today I belong to being alive!'

He wiped the fog where it dribbled like tears down his cheeks then climbed down to take the tiller once more and work on the lines.

*I'll bait this one with gar now there's more light for the fish to see it and leave the lure on the other one.* Attaching new hooks to the line took only a few minutes' work with the pliers. Christos stuck the hooks into the wooden reel and stowed it. Then he threw the bucket over the side. When it was full he dragged it back by the lanyard and washed the blood off the kill-pit deck. The water sluiced out through the self-drainers.

*It'll only get dirty again but it's easier to wash when it's still wet.* His father always said it was safer and more shipshape too.

'Blood's slipperier than water – it's twice as bloody dangerous,' he'd say, chuckling at his own lame pun. Satisfied with his clean deck, Christos stowed the bucket.

*There's nothing to do now, Chris old son, but sit back, take the weight off, and wait – again.*

The fog was broken now, rolling itself back into towering white eiderdowns. It seemed to burn off from the surface of the sea only to reassemble itself into huge clouds floating in a blue sapphire sky. Surface currents drifted like snail trails, meandering across the unrippled blue. Days like these were so beautiful that Christos felt a pain through his body, as though a hook pierced the core of him. He wished he knew enough words to say how beautiful the world was.

*Could it be any better, even if she was here?* Christos listened to the motor putt-putting until he realised he was actually waiting for *Li'l Bit* to reply. He laughed aloud at himself, then laughed aloud at the day, shouted aloud at the sun, until he was there, cutting the motor as they coasted into the beach on Hummocky Island.

His father had never let him explore Hummocky before, although he'd circumnavigated it by sea and seen its black rocks and sea caves. He'd always wanted to climb the hills at either end too.

*First – work, Chris! Clean the fish, anchor* Li'l Bit, *set up camp, then you can look around.*

The cove on the leeward side shone white and beckoning as the dory crunched onto the coral sand. Christos jumped over the side like a pirate on Treasure Island, anchor in hand and filleting knife in his waistband. He buried the anchor spades into the sand, pushing them in with his foot, then tied the rope off short.

*I'll anchor her in the bay later; for now it's better to be safe than sorry. I've had enough surprises today without Li'l Bit drifting off and leaving me marooned.*

Christos pulled off the for'ard hatch cover and put it down on the beach. Reaching into the icebox, he heaved out his fish, laying them on top of it. Even before his first trip to sea he remembered filleting fish and skinning the fillets with his mother. He was only young then, but the smell of cut fish flesh still reminded him of those times with her.

Inserting the point of his knife into the vent of the biggest mackerel, Christos made a quick slit straight up to the head.

*I'll just gut them and leave the heads on. Then they can see for themselves what size they are!* He began to imagine the looks of approval he'd get from everyone.

*I might be small but they'll have to think twice about what I can do if I go home with a boat full. That'll show them.* He'd always been a show-off. Christos remembered what his grandfather said once when he was showing off when he was little.

'Stop skiting. Too proud and you end up fall. Look twice as bad if you go head over the heels!'

But I can't stuff this up, Grandad. There's two ready for the box.

Working quickly Christos threw the guts and gills into the bucket, where they slapped against the plastic sides like hands against wet flesh. The doggie was far smaller and easier to handle. He had it cleaned in no time.

I can do this with one arm tied behind my back! He washed the blood from the carcasses and the hatch cover in the clean waves before slipping the clean fish back into the icebox. A hungry seagull moved in to pick at the leftovers. Pulling his food bag out of the for'ard hatch, Christos laid it on the dry sand above the highwater mark, then grabbed the full gut-bucket and hoisted it back into the kill-pit. He tried to push *Li'l Bit* to sea but she stuck fast.

I've only been ashore half an hour and she's high and dry. There's a four-metre drop in this tide, old mate. You'd better get a wriggle on. Christos pulled the anchor from the sand and placed it on board.

He put his hands on *Li'l Bit*'s bow and pushed. The dory didn't move. He pushed again, this time as hard as he could, his feet digging deep into the sand. Nothing. *Li'l Bit* was beautifully balanced and light in the water, but as heavy as lead out of it. Christos knew he was in trouble if she really was beached. He'd never move her by himself.

*If she's stuck I'll have to wait for eight or nine hours to float her and I won't be able to fish the incoming tide. That'll spoil everything! I might catch anything on the reef: mackerel, yes, but maybe a red emperor or even a coral trout. Dad'll be so proud if I get onto some big money fish. But I won't be doing anything if she's stuck.*

Christos squatted down under *Li'l Bit*'s bow and lifted with his legs, pushing back as hard as he could. Still nothing. He rocked her from side to side, his legs quivering with the exertion. Sweat started on his forehead. *Li'l Bit* moved – just a bit but there was some hope. Christos timed another shove with an incoming wave. It helped lift her weight and she moved again.

A few more shoulder nudges together with the waves and *Li'l Bit* floated back to sea.

*You are so lucky, mate!*

Christos grabbed the anchor rope so the dory didn't get away and sucked in some deep breaths. He took off his shirt and threw it back onto the dry beach. It was hot and he was in a hurry. He pushed off hard, throwing his legs up onto the deck as he did so. *Li'l Bit* scooted out to sea, light as a seagull again. Christos made his way to the stern, uncoiling the knotted rope he used to climb aboard. He threw the loose end over the side to use later. Then he waited as the tide and current took the dory away from the shore. When she was far enough out he emptied the fish guts and gills, watching them drift slowly to the bottom. Little fish and all sorts of small reef animals began to nibble and tear, feasting on the mess of flesh and entrails. Christos watched, fascinated.

*I suppose I eat dead things too, everything that's alive eats dead things. Dead fish, dead plants, dead chickens, dead cattle – they're alright. But eating dead guts is a bit much, even for me.*

Further out he set the anchor. The water was so window-glass clear that it looked shallow, no more than a couple of metres, but the chain and rope proved it was closer to twelve. When he was satisfied with the length of rope, he tied it off on the Samson post. Christos stood up, looking back to the island, breathing in the warm morning air. The fog was still lifting but already it was a day to die for.

*Maybe I won't get to explore the whole island in one day. It's bigger than I remember. Maybe I'll come back with Karis and we can explore together.* What they might explore alone on an island made him blush, not with shame, but with anticipation.

*I'm daydreaming too much. It's time to get going.* Christos breathed the salted air down deep into his lungs, dived into the crystalline water, and swam ashore.

# CHAPTER 5

It was afternoon when Christos woke up in his camp under the she-oak trees. He sat up quickly and looked at his watch.

*Three p.m. It feels later. I slept for almost two and a half hours.* Sweat had matted his hair as he'd dozed under the casuarinas. He shook his head like a tired dog. He'd dreamed about whales. One of them had lifted its tail and smashed the ...

*Li'l Bit!* Christos panicked, jumping up and running to the top of the dune to look out to sea. *What if I've lost* Li'l Bit? But the dory rode at anchor right where he'd left her. He'd had all the dramas he needed today.

*Calm down, it was a dream.* He walked slowly back to camp, wiping drool from the corner of his mouth.

He'd been hungry after he'd explored the north end of the island. It was a long climb. The hill was much higher than he guessed. It had taken a long time but the view was spectacular across the islands to the blue mountains on the mainland.

'I'm king of my birthday,' he said sitting down for a rest on a small cairn of stones someone had thoughtfully piled on top of his castle.

There were a few boats in the bay. Here and there he could make out shoals of bait with a following of terns and seagulls diving from above, sometimes the surface of the sea around them broken by the flip of feeding bonita.

The sea caves were disappointing after that, just holes in the rock really. It was fun but ... it would have been better to share.

*How many times have I said that today? I should have asked someone.* But no one would have been allowed to come. His mother had said, 'A boy by himself is sensible, more than one is trouble. Besides, they're too young.' So that was settled.

*What would she have said if I'd asked if Karis could come?* He laughed aloud. *Not likely! I can still wish she was here though, can't I?*

After the climb he ate lunch – a big feed of salami and cheese sandwiches, and drained one of the water bottles. Lucky his mother had given him a spare. He collected wood for a fire but it was too hot to kindle it now.

*At least the wood will be ready for tonight.* He spread out his sleeping bag and hung his food bag up in a tree. Then he thought he'd just lie down for a tick in the she-oak shade. Two and a half hours ago. Christos rubbed his face. He felt groggy and sticky.

*A swim will do the trick.*

Christos took off his shirt and watch and hung them both from a casuarina branch.

*The breeze will dry the sweat. I'll smell a bit less when I put it back on.* He laughed. *Well, that's the idea anyway! I'll swim out to Li'l Bit, bring her in and get set to fish the sunset tide. Things are always better with a plan worked out.*

Christos ran up over the dune and out into the water, diving when he was thigh deep. It was cool, cold almost, and clean. The water cleared his head immediately. He felt alive again. *Li'l Bit* had swung at her anchor.

*The tide's going out now, almost on the turn. There must be a current that runs round the bay. She's swung to the south and closer to shore.* Christos trod water for a while as he washed his face properly, ducking his head under a few times to wet his hair so he could push it back flat against his skull. He felt like a seal with his black hair slicked back over his head and his brown skin. That's what his father always said, but his sisters reckoned he looked like a movie star with his blue eyes smouldering.

*Who am I to disagree with the ladies?* Christos smiled to himself as he struck out for *Li'l Bit*.

He was a good swimmer, thin and sleek, though his shorts slowed him down when the pockets filled with water, pulling them down his hips. As he swam he looked beneath him. There were all sorts of corals and fish that weren't common nearer the mainland. He decided to have a closer look.

*There's still plenty of time before I have to get fishing. I'll keep my eye on Li'l Bit so I know where I am and don't get swept out to sea.* When he got to the dory he reached up to hang from the anchor rope while he got his breath back. He tried to hoist his shorts with one hand but didn't get far so, after a quick look around, he pulled them off and threw them up into the kill-pit. He felt free, dressed only in his underpants, but he laughed at himself.

*Why look around? There's no one to see!* Christos sucked in a quick breath then duck-dived down into the deep water.

The coral was alive with fish and prawns and shells. He picked one up to look more closely, a big cowrie, but the animal inside disappeared before his hand touched it, as quick as an eyelid blinking.

But it was the colour of things that was the most amazing. Here everything seemed brighter; even the lazy rock cod, which looked muddy brown out of the water, were almost fluorescent orange here.

Christos glanced up to check that *Li'l Bit's* shadow was still above him. It was, and the day was so clear that above the dory he could see the huge grey-white clouds rolling through the sky. It made him giddy for a moment, as though he was hanging upside down like a kid with his knees hooked over a branch. He closed his eyes then looked down again to the familiar things turned on their heads. There was so much more he wanted to see, but he knew he'd have to surface soon to breathe.

*This coral's too deep to keep diving down to. It hurts my eyes.*

Christos searched for some reef to explore that was closer to the surface. There were a series of bommies to the north of *Li'l Bit*, following the reef in towards the shore.

*The tops of them must just about be out of the water by now, with the tide going out. Maybe it'd be easier to go up above to look? Walk around a bit? No shoes – stupid idea. Besides it's fun here under the sea. The bommies look like a row of flat-topped mushrooms from below. It's like being in some weird octopus's garden.* Christos saw the shadow of a big fish sheltering under the nearest one.

*Maybe it's a groper or a big cod or a huge coral trout. I'll go look. But first I need to breathe!*

Three quick strokes took him to the surface. Exhaling like a blowing whale, Christos sucked his breath in deeply as he swam to the back of the dory, hanging onto the rope that trailed over the transom as he balanced on top of the metal plate of the rudder. It was enough to give him a rest before he dived again.

He glanced at his watch but saw only his bare wrist.

*You idiot! You left it ashore.* As much fun as it was, he couldn't swim forever. It seemed as though at least half an hour had passed.

*But it can't have been that long. I only took a couple of breaths! I'll have to watch the sun. It disappears fast once it gets low. Don't want to miss good fishing time. Another quick dive and that's it. Then I'll catch a heap!*

Christos pushed off, swimming quickly to the closest bommie before he duck-dived down. It was unnerving being under the coral, like there was a stone tree growing above him – as though he was in some sort of underworld, with grass-like coral below his feet. The cod swam leisurely over to examine him. Christos put out his hand to feel its dappled side. It felt almost like human skin, hardly scaly at all, or maybe not human, more like a snake's. The cod's huge eye swivelled to look at him as it lazed past, close enough to touch him with its pectoral fins. Its half-opened mouth was big enough to swallow his head in one bite, but like most sea creatures it wasn't aggressive, just inquisitive. It swam slowly away, satisfied, it seemed, that he was neither food nor a threat.

*It's so big, so content.* A rush of belonging

filled him, followed almost as suddenly by a sense of shame that he would consider killing such a beautiful creature. But almost immediately he remembered the time he'd seen a cod swallowing another smaller one, snuffing out its life without so much as a blink of its bulging eyes.

*It's a cod-eat-cod world.* Christos laughed. He didn't mean to but he laughed aloud, his lungs getting a mouthful of water. Trying not to swallow any more sea he swam quickly to the surface.

Coughing and spluttering, Christos tried to control his breath, reaching out with his feet to grip onto the edge of the coral at the top of the bommie, but even without any waves the swell washed him against its hard, jagged edge, scraping at the skin on his chest.

*It's too dangerous here. There's nothing to hold onto properly. And it's almost time to fish. But there's one last thing to do.* He pushed off again for *Li'l Bit.* Grabbing hold of the transom rope, he balanced himself on the rudder. He could still taste acid in the back of his throat from coughing up water. He hated that feeling, almost like he had just vomited. He tried to get more spit into his mouth to ease the urge to cough again.

*I'll wait until it passes. I want this to be good.* He listened to the small wave-slaps against the side of the hull, the sound of the sea. It calmed him. He balanced for a while longer, listening. It was cold in the breeze so he sank down into the warm water, letting the swell lift his body, silk against his skin.

*Yes, I'll remember this day*, he thought as he took a deep breath and dived. *So I can tell her.*

Only a few metres under *Li'l Bit*, he pinched his nose and dived straight down beneath her hull. Now when he glanced forward above his head he saw only coral and rocks on the ocean floor. Looking back under his feet he saw the bottom of *Li'l Bit*'s hull and the sky beyond. It was the strangest of all experiences – the familiar world stood on its head – as though he was buried under a sky of rocks and coral that was the ocean floor. Christos let himself float feet first back up until his feet touched the bottom of the dory's keel.

*I'm walking on the bottom of the surface of the sea!* The clouds were immense below his feet. They seemed to rock, as though he was overbalancing, with every movement *Li'l Bit* made. His medallion fell down over the top of his head. Christos grabbed it, slipping it between his teeth.

*Mum will kill me if I lose it!* Then he steadied himself with his outstretched hands and, balancing like a tightrope walker, he walked along *Li'l Bit's* keel. His mind reeled at the sensations overwhelming him. He closed his eyes, surrendering to the water-world wrapped around him. Every old sensation was new, different, upside down. He totally lost his usual mind.

*My name's Karis. What's yours?*

He heard her ask again and again.

*Yes, I'll remember this.*

When he opened his eyes the sea was dark.

*That's not cloud-shadow. The sun's gone down a bit, but I know what a cloud-shadow's like. This is . . .*

They were on him then, around him, swirling like silver leaves caught in a spin of wind. Fish. Thousands upon thousands of baitfish schooled around him, all flashing their sides to the sun like silver foil.

*It's like magic. It's . . . it's . . .* he couldn't think of any words to describe yet another moment in his day of stunning moments.

*My name's Chris, I'll say and I'll hold out my hand to shake hers. Then she'll touch me electric.* Christos almost wept that she wasn't here.

He swam out from under the dory, the fish parting before him, forming a perfect cocoon exactly the shape of his body. He bobbed to the surface, gasping a huge breath before diving again into the dark mass of them. As he dived the fish parted once more, dividing before him. Christos rolled in a somersault and the fish rolled, always leaving a gap between his body and them which perfectly mimicked his every move. He rolled again and again, then swam parallel to the surface, wrapped like an Egyptian mummy. Christos allowed his body to sink until he stood vertically in mid-water. He stretched both his arms from his sides and straightened his legs. The fish formed a perfect cross around him.

But then, as suddenly as they had appeared, the fish were gone. All he could see was the edge of the school. Christos swam a few strokes to try to catch them up, but they moved too fast.

He glanced towards *Li'l Bit*.

*It's time to get fishing. Where there's bait there's* ... Even as he turned back to the dory a small school of Spanish mackerel flew past him like blue spears. In turn they sped forward, chopping at the edge of the school of bait. Eating those beautiful things which had danced with him. The water was full of a shrapnel of small fragments of flesh and gut.

*Got to catch one of those beauties. Get fishing, Chris.* He surfaced and swam to *Li'l Bit*.

*Quick, before they're gone.*

# CHAPTER 6

Christos grabbed the rope and hauled himself up over the side of the dory. Scrambling across the kill-pit, he threw open the engine hatch, knocked *Li'l Bit* out of gear, lifted the decompression valve, fitted the handle and started the motor on the second stroke.

*Beautiful, team!* He ran for'ard, dragging the anchor in, then jumped back into the kill-pit. Grabbing the gar from the icebox he slid down, panting, into the standing-pit.

The coaming was rough against his bare skin, reminding him he wasn't wearing any clothes. He thought about grabbing his shorts or going ashore to get his shirt and watch for as long as the split second it took to kick *Li'l Bit* into gear.

*You don't need a shirt to go fishing, and who needs a watch, I know what time it is – fishing time!* Even as *Li'l Bit* was still thinking about making way, Christos clipped on the transom line and started unrolling it over the stern. He steered the dory across the mouth of the bay, following the bait.

Christos clipped on the outrigger line and baited it with a gar, lowering it over the side before he grabbed the gloves. They passed the school to starboard. Christos checked over his shoulder to try and position *Li'l Bit* so they'd both pass exactly where he hoped the mackerel were feeding.

*Right on the sweet spot.*

The first fish struck the outrigger bait hard, yanking the dory to starboard. Christos let *Li'l*

*Bit* follow the Spaniard as it ran, trying to get some slack so he could pull the outrigger line over to the dory. He could barely manage it and he wasn't even trying to drag it in yet.

*This is a big fish. But I can handle it.*

*You hope you can!*

Christos grabbed the outrigger line. Just as his hand wrapped around it the mackerel jumped. It was forty metres from the boat, illuminated by the setting sun, flipping its body from side to side, desperate to flick the hooks from its mouth. The water glistened along its sides as if it was moulded from molten gold. It must be more than a metre long. Maybe forty kilos or bigger

*It weighs almost as much as I do. How good will it be if I can land it?* The thought spurred him on.

*Concentrate. You'll lose it if you don't play it.* The line fell limp as the fish jumped and Christos hauled it in as quickly as he could, taking up the slack the fish might use to whip the hook from its mouth. But before he could get a wrap the fish ran again. The cord leapt out of his hand and out of the line tray, flicking back onto the outrigger as it ran further to starboard. He steered *Li'l Bit* after it.

'Damn!' he swore.

*Don't run across the transom line or there'll be a huge tangle. I should get that line in and let the fish tire itself out pulling against the weight of the dory. I won't be able to drag it straight in. It's too big. There's not much light left either and besides, I can't handle more than this little beauty even if I hook-up another one. I'll have to take my chances and leave it run while I get the transom line in.* Christos could see the shockie on the outrigger straining like a rubber band about to snap. The line vibrated with tension, flicking water like dewdrops exploding from a fence wire hit by a stick.

He dragged in the transom line, hand over hand, throwing it all in a mess on the kill-pit floor.

*Deal with that later.* He was already puffed by the time he'd got the first line aboard.

*Now the real work begins.* Again Christos pulled in the line from the outrigger.

*Feels like a whale.* The fish was still fighting hard and running from side to side, each twist almost throwing him out of the standing-pit.

*There's no way I can hold this with my arms. I'm not strong enough. Maybe across my shoulders?* Christos leaned down, ducking his head under the straining cord. He stood unsteadily, taking the weight of the tight line across his back.

The thin cord sawed savagely across his shoulders. With each twist of the fighting fish he could feel the line cut deeper in. He wasn't bleeding but he was sure that he would be if the Spaniard kept the fight up.

*I can't do it like this either. Have to do something different, and fast. Why didn't I go back to get my shirt?*

'Wishing won't get you anywhere,' he heard his father's voice say. 'Do something!'

*My shorts! I can use them.* Christos lowered himself carefully then leaned into the kill-pit to grab his shorts. In one movement he lifted the line, slapped his shorts behind his neck, and lowered the cord onto the cloth.

*That's better. Much, much better.*

The line began to rise again. The Spaniard was preparing to jump. Christos loosened his left-hand grip and looked back, ready for action. Even as the Spaniard's head cleared the water he reefed in more line, straining out as far as he could to drag in long lengths. He grabbed seven, eight, nine lengths quickly into the tray.

The fish leapt, heading straight towards *Li'l Bit*. Christos grimaced, leaning hard against the side of the kill-pit, trying not to be pulled out. His shoulders screamed with pain. Arms turned to jelly.

*Can't stop. Not now.* He panted in time with his movement. In jagged, shallow, gasps.

He was down to the wire. Twenty metres.

*The fish'll keep fighting and I'll have to hold it on the trace. It'll cut.* He could feel the Spaniard going deep. But then, just as suddenly, it rose.

*What are you doing, fish? It's going to jump again.* Christos sucked in a deep breath before the Spaniard jumped, or tried to, twenty metres from the dory. Only half-cleared the surface.

The sun was gone but he saw now its steel-grey magnificence. Beautiful, but dog-tired already from the fight.

*Makes two of us.* Exhausted as he was, Christos pulled on the line again. Five more metres, six, seven; and then it dived straight down deep. Straining. Slicing the darkening sea. Christos couldn't hold it with one hand. He wrapped both hands, holding the line like a waterskier. But he couldn't stop the fish. It sank down, heading under the transom. Closer to the propeller.

*No! No! I can't lose it like that.* But Christos couldn't pull the fish up. He could feel the sweat running like tears from his temples and down across his cheeks.

*I will win. Hold on. I'll beat it. I'll show them.* With a desperate effort he threw himself backwards, jerking the line up as hard as he could. Suddenly the fish fell still.

'No! I've lost it!' he gasped. But he could still feel the weight, even heavier than before. The fish seemed to be lying still in the water, moving out from under them as *Li'l Bit* drove forward.

He couldn't believe his luck. He'd heard of this happening before.

*The hooks jag up through the roof of the fish's mouth and pierce its brain. Dead! Never thought it was true. You know fishermen. Don't let the truth stand in the way of a good story.* If he could have, Christos would have laughed. But he had no strength for anything but the fish. His eyes were misty with sweat, making the darkness seem deeper than it was.

*Wait till I show Dad tomorrow. What a fish! But stop skiting! You haven't got it on ice yet.* Christos pulled in easier line over the stern as the fish rose to the surface, following behind *Li'l Bit* like an obedient dog. He pulled it in until the fish swam beside the dory. By then he was almost spent. This was easily the biggest mackerel he'd ever seen.

*Won't be able to get it over the side, even with both hands. Need the gaff. If I can get the front half of it over the edge I should be able to slip it into the kill-pit.* Christos was woozy with exertion. He had to do it now. His hands shook as he grabbed the gaff. He could hardly free it from its bracket on the edge of the kill-pit.

*Now for the final lift!* Christos wiped the sweat from his eyes with the back of one arm, dropped his shorts into the kill-pit, then breathed deeply a few times. He gripped the gaff in both his hands and went down, leaning over the side, to claim his prize.

As he jagged the gaff into the Spaniard's flesh behind the pectoral fin he saw it. Something. Black on black. A shadow rising from the depths towards him. Before he could throw himself out of the way he saw its jaws open, its teeth only a gaff handle away. Shark's teeth in a serrated circle, fifty centimetres in diameter. Triangular teeth curved sideways like razor blades straining from its mouth as it tried to fit more fish in. It thrust up from underwater, sawing its grey head from side to side, water spraying from its feeding frenzy. A tiger shark was slicing his fish in two.

Christos screamed in shock, hurling himself backwards into the standing-pit. Gaff still in his hands, he dragged only two-thirds of his mighty fish into the dory with him. Maybe fifteen kilos gone in one bite. Christos landed half in the standing-pit, half out. His heart slammed. His aching arms lost their tiredness. *Li'l Bit* steered wild.

Dropping the gaffed Spaniard in the kill-pit, Christos struggled to get back into the standing-pit. But it was too late. With the sound of galvanised iron tearing from a roof in a cyclone, *Li'l Bit* lurched forward. Her nose reared up out of the water like a horse about to jump. Christos was flung forward by the impact, landing in the kill-pit. His heart pounded. He staggered to his knees. In the last grey light he saw that he'd run aground on one of the coral bommies he'd swum under less than an hour before.

*Li'l Bit* strained forward, her motor thrusting, forcing the bow up, the transom down.

*Have to stop the motor. It's forcing her stern underwater, where the shark* ... He threw up the motor hatch and reefed up the decompression lever. Wasn't the best way to do it but the motor died.

*What now? What next?* In the failing light Christos could see the shore less than a hundred and fifty metres away.

*Might as well be a thousand. I can't walk on water.* Then he saw the shark surface again ... waiting for the next bite. Scrambling up the angled deck to the for'ard hatch, Christos opened it and dived inside.

# CHAPTER 7

It was dark under the deck. Christos lay sprawled across the anchor rope.

*What'll I do? How's Li'l Bit stuck? Is she sinking?* He sat up quickly in the darkness and scrabbled frantically along both sides of her hull, feeling for holes. Nothing.

*But she might be holed further down. Can't tell. Did she ride up here on top of a swell? Don't know – wasn't watching. Maybe another swell will lift her off?* His heart pounded at his ears as he gulped for breath like a stranded fish.

*Calm down. You've seen a shark before. Yeah, but I've never been stuck on a bommie at night with a shark out there that knows there's a feed on board. If she's holed ... if I lose her!* Christos held his breath but it was no good, he could only hear his heart.

*Calm down. What'll I do? A fisherman without a boat's like a crab without its shell. You have to think, Chris.*

*Idiot! Idiot! Idiot! The third time today. I was supposed to watch where I was going. Now look at the mess I'm in.*

'Sorry, girl,' he told *Li'l Bit*, patting her hull repeatedly as though she could feel his reassurance. 'It's my fault!'

*The fish must have dragged me in a huge circle. Well, it wasn't the fish's fault, I steered after it to take the strain off the line. Idiot!* His father would never forgive him for not watching where he was going.

*Maybe Mum's right. I'm not old enough, or strong enough, or smart enough. I can't do it. Can't do anything right. I'm not a fisherman. Not even* a *fisherman's little finger.* He lay down among the coils of anchor rope, trying to bury himself under them.

Christos wiped his fringe back from his face with shaking hands. He felt like crying, but held himself back. He was shocked, angry, frustrated, disappointed in turn. And his hands and feet were freezing. His teeth chattering. He couldn't stop them knocking in his mouth.

*It must be shock, like people in car accidents get. Or it might be because I'm not wearing any clothes! And I've got nothing warm to put on either. It'll be colder than this later tonight.*

*Idiot!* he ranted at himself. *You should have been prepared. You should have got your shirt.*

He could hear his father's voice, almost see his face peering out of the darkness. '*That's your problem, Chris, you always go off half-cocked.*' He could see that sort of smirk his father wore.

*This time he's right. But he isn't always. All the other dories have emergency flares on board for times like this, but not Li'l Bit. The old man thinks accidents are caused by fools, that Li'l Bit wouldn't ever get into any sort of trouble and need help like I need it right now.*

'The sea is kind to the careful,' his father said. 'And you can't be too careful at sea.'

*I've let everybody down.* Christos huddled closer, trying to warm himself under the rope. It was no good though, he'd have to find something else to cover himself.

*The lifejacket!*

*There are no flares, but the lifejacket's stowed under the bow! It won't keep me very warm but I should wear it anyway in case I need to swim.* Christos stopped that thought. He couldn't, wouldn't think about being in the water right now.

*Li'l Bit won't let me down. We're a team. I'll worry about the rest of ... everything else later. Now I need to get warm.* He felt under the deck. The lifejacket was tied along the side of the hull. His hands found it in the darkness but his fingers couldn't untie the rope. He fumbled with it for a minute, but couldn't see the knot. Didn't know what knot it was by touch. A real fisherman would know and be able to tie and untie it in the dark.

*But Dad's not here. Do it yourself, Chris. You got yourself into this, you'll have to get yourself out. Maybe I can cut the rope? No knife. It's at the other end of the dory. Well, I'll have to get it then.*

Christos thought about crossing the deck in the darkness. For the first time since the accident, he was forced to think about the shark. He'd seen lots of sharks before, but that was during the day, and he was with his father.

*It's different, being alone. I don't want to go out there. Not keen at all.* He sat back, knees to his chest, his arms wrapped tight around them.

*You have to think straight, Chris. You've had a fright but you're all right now.*

He could hear the motor ticking as it cooled down, felt the breeze wafting in from above, the last of the evening north-easterly.

*Of course! That's something. That'll help.* Christos reached out carefully onto the deck until he found the hatch cover. Grabbing it as firmly as he could, he kneeled and slipped it back into place. With the lid closed the heat of the motor was trapped inside and the breeze didn't blow on him either. He coughed at the strong smell of diesel and oil under the deck, but he shivered less.

*I can put up with the fumes if I stay warm.*

'There you go. One thing done, and it's a good thing,' he told *Li'l Bit.*

*Time to think some more. Maybe I could start the motor at different times through the night? The heat'll keep me warm. But to start Li'l Bit I'll have to go out on deck. If the choice is that or freeze, I'll do it. Good. Another idea I can use.*

*Now about the lifejacket. I need the torch to see with.*

He knew that he could get the knot undone if he really wanted to, if he was calm enough, but he knew too that the real reason he wanted the torch was to make the coming night more bearable. He had stowed it under the deck beside the standing-pit with all the tools.

*If I've got it, at least I'll be able to see something and maybe with the pliers I can . . .*

A wave, bigger than the others, slapped against the side of the dory. It rose and fell against her hull.

*Will this wave be enough to lift her free?* He waited, breath held, but *Li'l Bit* stayed held tight. His thoughts turned unwillingly back to the shark.

*It'll still be out there. It just ate a meal. It'll do what all sharks do – wait, hoping for more.*

Christos sat upright on the keel, in the centre of the boat, not touching the hull.

*It's so thin, the plywood, all there is between me and it.* He could almost feel the shark cruising through the water.

*If Li'l Bit's hull wasn't between us I could lean out and touch it.* He wrapped his arms around himself, trying not to think at all.

*Usually sharks are just a nuisance, taking half of every fish or busting the gear until you move to another spot to get away from them. But it's different now.* He kept picturing it in his mind's eye. He could almost feel the water move like a black silk sheet, parting for the shark to glide through.

He felt as though it could smell him. He knew that sharks had acute sensors for picking up electromagnetic impulses.

'They can sense a fish quiver a kilometre away,' Mr Walls, his Science teacher, said. 'They can sense the impulses caused by a human brain thinking from half that distance.' Mr Walls looked at Christos. 'That means you'll be safe, Chris. No impulses in your brain!'

'No brain, no strain!' one of his mates added. And another called out, 'All his impulses are down lower, sir!'

Christos shot the kid a dirty look.

*But it's one time I can remember being really interested in school, when we dissected the shark in Biology.* He could almost feel the slice of flesh under his scalpel.

*Now the tables are turned. Li'l Bit's hull's as thin as an eggshell and I'm the chicken inside. A chicken waiting for the carving knife.*

'They can smell, well, at least follow the scent of blood, or oil,' Mr Walls said. Christos remembered his bleeding, half-eaten fish in the kill-pit; its juices would be draining out through the self-drainers into the sea.

*The shark won't go away while it can smell that. I need to put the fish in the icebox and wash the kill-pit down, but that means getting out on deck. There's no way I'm going outside without a torch!*

But he was feeling better now, not shivering so much. Things were starting to make more sense. Nothing seemed as urgent as before. The motor gave off a lot of heat, but he could still feel the breeze luffing in from the open standing-pit hatch.

*I'll be even warmer if I close that too. I still don't know how Li'l Bit's stuck. I might be able to get her off the coral. I know she's heavy, but most of her weight must still be floating, mustn't it? Maybe if I rock her from side to side she might slip free?*

'What do you think?' he asked. Christos knew he was talking to the dory again. *But you're almost alive, aren't you, Li'l Bit. Besides, right now you're my only friend.* Her smooth-skinned hull, the water lapping against her side, her motor like a heart that would beat to keep him warm.

It wasn't *Li'l Bit*'s fault that he'd driven her to this.

'I'd better find out how you're stuck first, before I do anything else. I don't want to make it worse.' Rocking the boat might hole her if she wasn't already.

*If she is sinking I should hear water. Even if I can't see it, I should be able to hear where it's coming in.* Christos put his ear against the plywood between her ribs. The sea lapped against her hull like a cat at a saucer of milk.

*Wait!* He could just make out the sound of the plywood creaking, groaning as a swell moved the dory ever so slightly. But there was no sound of water running. Christos took a deep breath, letting it out slowly.

'Good for you, *Li'l Bit*!' He smiled. The dory was certainly stuck but he was convinced now that she wasn't sinking.

*Knowing that still doesn't get you out of here though, does it? You need a plan. If you have a plan everything will be better.* Just the thought of doing something, one step at a time, slowly and methodically, ordered his thoughts. His breath slowed and he could feel the steady tadump-tadump of his heart.

*Now . . . what are the facts? First, the tide is still going out. Maybe Li'l Bit will slip off the coral as the tide drops?* He couldn't count on it but it was one idea.

*That is, if she isn't completely wedged into the heads of coral like a fish in a crab's claw. Maybe she's caught by the keel? Then she won't move at all. One thing's for certain, I'll only find out how she's stuck by looking, and to look I'll need the torch.*

*Second, if I wait long enough, the tide will come in. If the low tide doesn't slide Li'l Bit free then the high tide should pop her up like a cork. Surely? Either way all I have to do is wait. I'm always waiting for something!* Christos smiled grimly.

*It'll be at least two hours for the tide to turn, then another three for it to be back to the height it was when I ran aground. Maybe a couple of hours more until she floats off. Seven hours at the most. Less than most days at school — counting footy training. That's the plan then. I'll wait.* His whole body sagged with relief.

*Now, all I have to do is decide what to do while I'm sitting here! I still need the torch. No, I want the torch and I like the idea of getting my fish out of the kill-pit so it doesn't keep leaking juice into the sea. Maybe the shark'll clear off if it can't smell anything, and I wouldn't mind grabbing my shorts either.*

'You almost smiled then,' Christos said aloud. 'Didn't he, *Li'l Bit?*'

'Stop looking at me,' he continued. 'I can't help being in me jocks!' He laughed and it came gurgling from him like water from a rain-filled gutter. He laughed until his tiny world felt better.

For the first time, almost as though he'd woken from a bad dream, Christos was able to concentrate enough to remember catching the fish.

*It's quite a mackerel, whether it's intact now or not. Actually, it's a great fish! I'll carry it over my shoulder up to the Co-op so everyone can see how big it is. They'll all 'oooh' and 'aaah'.* He could almost see her smiling. His father would thump his back, and his mother would wink, like she did when he'd done something good. Even the other fishermen would have to say what a great fish it was.

*I'm still not keen, though, on going out across the deck to put it away. Don't care if I'm not game. I don't have to so I won't.*

But then the idea struck him.

*I could crawl to the stern under the deck of the kill-pit. The deck's low but I'm small enough.* He'd done it once before when he was younger and his father dropped a bolt into the bilge.

*I could slide through, belly against the hull, down past the motor, under the kill-pit and the icebox and pop up into the standing-pit. Then I can come back the same way without ever going out on deck. I'll get the torch, the cleaning knife and my shorts and, if the coast's clear, I'll jump out and slip the fish into the icebox. It'll only take a minute.*

Christos tried to convince himself he wasn't a total chicken – not that anyone would ever find out unless he told them. The shock was wearing off but he still wasn't keen on being out on the deck in the dark. But the wait would be that much easier to take if he had some light, and the knife would be some protection, if the worst came to the worst. He almost felt like crying again, but this time with relief.

'That's it, *Li'l Bit*,' he said. 'We're going to be all right.' Christos thumped the plywood hull. 'Get a feed somewhere else!' he yelled at the shark. But even as his fist thudded against the wood, he wished he hadn't done it.

*That vibration just let the shark know you're still here. Why not just call it up on the phone? I know you've had a shock but think, mate!*

'There's no use crying over spilt milk,' he heard his mother's voice say. 'You can't take it back now it's done.'

Christos listened intently but he could hear only the lilt of water against *Li'l Bit*'s side. He had to get back to his plan.

*I need to co-ordinate everything. When I get to the standing-pit I'll need the torch first, to see what*

*I'm doing. Then I'll need the cleaning knife and maybe the pliers and . . . No, they can come later. Next I'll hop into the kill-pit, put my fish into the icebox and get my pants. Then I grab the bucket, wash the deck and put everything into it to carry back. Maybe if I go over the deck on the way back it'll be easier. It'll be quicker at least. If I do that, though, I'll have to open the for'ard hatch cover before I start. Then if anything happens I can dive into it – like a mud-skipper down its hole.* Christos felt safer having an escape planned.

*You can do this, no worries, Chris.*

He sat for a moment, making sure he pictured exactly the sequence of events once he got to the standing-pit.

'Right then, *Li'l Bit.* I'm ready!' He knelt and carefully pushed the hatch cover upward. Once it was open he slipped it forward along the deck until only the edge of it sat on the coaming. It was much lighter inside the hull now. He'd grown used to the total darkness under *Li'l Bit*'s deck. Christos knelt looking up at the stars.

With a pang of homesickness, or maybe loneliness, he remembered that his brothers and sisters would be sleeping now.

*Mum will be getting ready for Sunday, maybe reading her latest book before she goes to bed.* His body slumped.

*And where's Dad? Has he caught any fish?* But most he wondered what Karis was doing.

*Does she ever even think about me? Will she be proud of me when I come home? Or will it be too hard for her to hear that I could so easily have come to grief? Sometimes girls are like that. Like Mum when I was knocked out that time at football. When I woke up seeing two of everything Mum was there above me, laughing and crying.*

*'You're too small for this, Chris. You could have been killed!' Crying and laughing.*

*I couldn't hold my head up straight, it was lolling around like a rag doll, but I was okay.*

*'But I wasn't killed, Mum. I'm all right.' I remember glancing down the sideline and ... It was Karis I saw there, wasn't it? It was her on the sideline.*

He'd only just remembered it now.

*She was staring at me with that look on her face. Like she was worried about me. She glanced away as soon as I caught her eye. No, maybe you just want to remember it that way, Chris. Maybe you're just making it up?*

*Well, if I'm making it up I wish I wasn't. There's so much to tell her, so many things. When I get home I'll ask her if she wants to hang out with me.*

Christos looked up through the open hatch.

'When I do, let her say yes,' he asked the stars.

Then it was time.

# CHAPTER 8

Christos lay on his stomach, inching his way aft.

*No way I could do this with a lifejacket on. I'm a lot bigger now than the last time.* Sweat dribbled down his forehead.

*Maybe I should just go back up on deck? No, it's not far.* He stopped. Feeling around in the darkness, he located the side of the motor. It was still hot. He pulled his hand away quickly.

*Not even halfway.* He lay flat to catch

his breath and felt water on the tips of his outstretched fingers.

*What the hell is that?* He panicked. *What if Li'l Bit's taking water at the stern? What if I get further down and the bilge is full and I can't turn around? I'll have to take a breath and plunge in. But what if I get stuck? I'll drown.*

He tried to stop himself.

*Don't think about bad stuff. This was your idea. You could have gone across the deck if you weren't such a sook. You can do this. You will do it. I say you will.*

Christos lunged forward. Pushing hard with his legs in a burst of movement, he thrust his whole body under the kill-pit floor, his arms stretched before him like a diver.

*Now there's no choice, even if my worst nightmares are true.* Christos felt his way forward with his fingers. In the enclosed space he couldn't use his elbows so he pushed frog-wise with his feet. His breath laboured and he coughed oil and diesel fumes.

*Not far now. Taste the fresh air?* His

outstretched hands confirmed there wasn't much water. Just the normal bilge water all run down to the stern.

*It's just your mind playing tricks. Don't listen. You'll be right, mate.*

With a final push through the oily water Christos reached up to grab the lip of the hatch coaming. Pulling himself into a sitting position on the standing-pit floor, he sat panting in the clean air. But he kept his head below deck, out of shark range, just in case. He felt around for the torch. His hand locked onto it, flicking the switch even before he fully grasped it.

Light! Light flooded the standing-pit. At last he could see. His fears disappeared like shadows at midday. It was such a small thing, but the torch made all the difference. 'Thank you. Thank you,' he said, holding tight to Saint Christopher on his chain. His voice was strong. He felt stronger too, more confident, filled with light.

*Just stick to the plan. It's all worked this far.*

With the torch Christos could see the transom was nearly half-submerged.

*When I get out I'll only be half a gaff handle from the stern and a few handwidths away from the sea. An easy lunge for a shark. I'll have to be quick when I get there. Out of the standing-pit, into the kill-pit, then out of reach. You know you can do it, mate. The plan won't fail. There's a place for everything and everything is in its place.* But speed would be of the essence.

Christos tried to pull the filleting knife free from the basket. It was stuck.

*Damn! I'll take the lot then.* Quickly he emptied the contents of the storage basket into the bucket. Knives, pliers, leads, lures, evil eyes, sprag wire, all cascaded in a jangle of metal.

*Wouldn't it be easier to forget the fish and just crawl back under the deck right now?* But he dismissed the idea.

*It's my fish. I want to show it off to them tomorrow. Besides, I've got the torch now and I want my shorts too. If I die I want to die with some dignity!* Christos smiled weakly at the thought. But there were practical reasons as well.

*Even if I don't die it's uncomfortable in the nude,*

*the anchor rope hurts my bum and besides, my pants will keep me a bit warmer.* Christos smiled again, properly this time. What a difference the torch made.

The bucket was already full before he realised he'd stuffed up his plan.

*It's supposed to be empty so I can get the water to wash down the deck. Too late. Plan change. Take the bucket like it is, put the fish in the icebox and dump the gear in the for'ard hatch. You can wash down the deck later. Okay.*

Christos pushed the hatch cover into the kill-pit. The bucket followed.

*Go!* He jumped out of the standing-pit.

The torch beam shone wild across the dark face of the sea. Nothing broke the surface. Only a thousand facets of black waves sparkling back reflections of the torchlight.

*Maybe I can see how she's stuck?* But he couldn't bring himself to lean over to look into the sea beside the hull. He would be too close to the water. Besides, there was no need. No water in the bilge meant she certainly wasn't sinking.

*First things first. I can check out how she's stuck later.* Christos grabbed his shorts and threw them in the bucket before jamming the hatch cover back in place. Then he turned his attention to the fish. Its size shocked and pleased him. Now he got a good look at it, it was even bigger than he remembered. Not that he'd had much time to look.

*It's the biggest mackerel ever in our family! Even with a third of it missing you can still see it's bigger than any photograph of Dad or Grandad with their prize fish.*

For a moment Christos felt both angry and sad that the shark had torn such a huge mouthful of flesh away, spoiling his fish's beauty.

*Still, Dad'll have to agree it's bigger than anything he's ever caught.*

Christos looked at his two-thirds fish with a new rush of pride.

*Well, anyway, at least now it'll fit in the icebox!* He quickly placed the torch on the kill-pit floor and tried to pull the hooks from the fish's mouth. But when he bent down, he blocked the light.

*Damn!* Christos moved the torch to the other side of the deck, his fingers yanking at the hooks. He glanced up to check if anything was out there. The fish kept slipping towards the stern, between him and the sea. Christos slipped too. Working at this angle was difficult enough without the kill-pit floor being covered with loose line. He slipped, dropping the fish again. It slipped under the coils of transom line. He tried to shake it out clean but the fish was slippery and he was in a hurry. The two lines tangled into an unholy mess.

*Damn! Sort it out later.* Finally he stood up, pulling the fish free from where it had fallen into the wire and cord at his feet.

*Too much noise. Get on with it, mate!* But he still couldn't see what he was doing and only succeeded in getting his foot caught in the mess of lines. His hands were full so he tried to kick free but slipped again. *Get the fish sorted first and deal with the damn line later.*

*Only one thing for it.* He spun around to face away from the stern, placed the torch on the engine hatch cover and held the fish up in the light.

*That's better.* But his back was turned to the sea. The hairs rose on his neck.

*Steady, mate! Concentrate! Only a few seconds and it'll be safe on ice.*

He tried the hooks with the pliers but they were embedded deep in the bony top of the fish's mouth. Christos glanced over his shoulder at the moving sea.

*Hurry.* He could hear his heart thumping. *Hooks don't matter. Just throw the fish in with the line still attached. Dump it in the icebox and get out of here.*

Christos heaved the fish up, the gaff still stuck in its side. He pulled it out, struggling to half-carry, half-slide the fish up the deck to the icebox. He glanced quickly over his shoulder, then back.

*Damn! Should have lifted the lid first. Hurry!* He tried to open the icebox with one hand but couldn't. Glanced anxiously over his shoulder. The torchlight reflected off the mirrored waves.

He tried to balance the fish on the edge of the engine hatch but only succeeded in knocking the torch down into the kill-pit. Christos turned to grab the torch but slid down the dew-wet deck with the fish still in his arms. And then it was there.

In the torch's half-light Christos watched transfixed as the shark raised its massive head from the water and slid its grey-striped weight onto the transom. One flat eye caught the light. It seemed to be searching for him. With a crack as though her back was breaking, *Li'l Bit* lurched downwards. Christos fell. The starboard side of the transom dipped further below the surface. *Li'l Bit* couldn't save him this time. Christos felt himself twist, then fall inexorably towards the head of the inquisitive shark.

He threw the fish out in front of him.

'Go away!' he screamed, his voice thin and helpless. The startled tiger shark reacted, biting at its attacker. Christos could do nothing. Its jaws crushed closed on an unexpected mouthful of fish, missing his arm by centimetres, slashing the palm of his hand as it ripped the mackerel from his grip.

Christos fell. He could see the huge splash, felt the boat shudder as, with an almighty effort, the shark rolled itself back into the water, still grasping its meal of fish. Christos landed half on and half over the transom. Clutching at the deck, he dragged himself back on board, scrambling to get back to the safety of the for'ard hatch. But the tangled outrigger line snared his leg, and he was pulled out of the kill-pit. Out, down, overboard. He fought, clawing for a hold, but his legs flicked out over the side and he was gone, following the diving shark in a rush of water down into the ocean's black.

A halo of torchlight shone above him. Below was pitch darkness, except for the phosphorescence of a thousand animals feeding in the night, like a cathedral of stars in a nightmare sky. A shimmering, glowing world of animals feeding on the dead things that drifted down into their sunken city.

An image of *Li'l Bit*, drifting, flashed into his mind.

*They'll find my torch in the kill-pit and my camp, with my shirt and watch hanging where I left them, but I'll be gone, extinguished.*

His fingers clutched vainly at the unclutchable water. The line dragged him down after the shark. Deep down. Forcing water up his nose. Coughing. Drowning. He fought, flailing and choking.

Then suddenly there was nothing. The rush of water stopped. The shark was gone.

*Where are you?* Christos shook his leg violently, kicking at the huge knot of line with his loose foot, panic now overtaken by the complete calm they say comes the moment before death.

*I won't give up like this!* He twisted, kicking now with both his feet, loosening the tangle of line, kicking his way free, struggling towards the surface.

*Where is it? When will it come?* He could almost feel the shark circling towards him in the black water beneath. Breaking free of the surface with a sob of air, he swam three strokes towards the safety of the torchlight.

*Save me*, Li'l Bit! Even as he slid his stomach onto her deck, Christos saw the outrigger line tighten, dipping the transom deeper, dragging *Li'l Bit* down. Then, with a crack like a gunshot, the outrigger snapped in two, tearing both the lines and their cleats clean from the deck.

Christos's mind couldn't register what had happened. He worked like a machine, scrambling into the kill-pit, grabbing the bucket and torch. But it was too much, then, too much. Panic overwhelmed him. He vomited water across the engine cover, staggering, coughing and crawling up the deck. The torch beam arced through the night. Reaching the open hatch he dropped down onto the anchor rope, dragging the bucket and torch with him, vomit still drooling from his lips. With a final effort he reached out and threw the cover into place, forcing the hatch closed. His heart became the sound of him, and sobbing.

'Leave me alone! Get back! Get back!' he screamed between gasping breaths. 'Get!' Waving his arms as though fighting a childhood nightmare.

Torchlight filled *Li'l Bit*'s insides.

*It's warm here. I'm safe. It's over ...* Unexpectedly Christos was alive. Beyond all hope.

But his mind teetered in shock.

He curled himself into a ball between the coils of anchor rope. Fatigue and fear flooded his mind until they were too much for it to hold. Shivering uncontrollably, he blacked out, and the terror was gone.

# CHAPTER 9

It wasn't the sound of water lapping against the outside of the hull that was the first thing Christos heard when he woke. It was the sound of water slopping inside. He held his eyes closed tight.

*It can't be water. It can't. It isn't.* He was shivering, pain in every muscle. He had no idea how long he'd been unconscious but he did know it was long enough to get very cold. Cold and groggy. His mind was a fog of half-remembered images.

Water / Fish / Water / Eye / Teeth / Water / Screaming / Darkness / Water / Waiting / Swimming / Crawling / Vomiting / Darkness

He couldn't think about it. His stomach ground into a knot and he felt like vomiting again.

'Where are you?' he whispered, wishing his father was here now.

*Dad would know what to do.* He moved his body and his back spasmed with pain. Tried moving his legs. More pain. Christos forced his eyes to open.

*The torch is still shining, however long I've been asleep.* The light hurt his eyes. A headache beat at the inside of his brain. Christos closed his eyes but IT came at him out of the darkness. His eyes snapped open again. Everything was different now.

He felt so tired. He just wanted to go back to sleep, but he dared not close his eyes in case IT came for him. Without moving his throbbing head Christos searched along the hull. About a third down her starboard side, a few handwidths up from the bottom, a huge bulge staved in the plywood.

*One of her ribs is cracked, but not broken. It wasn't like that before. I would have felt it. The weight of the shark must have rolled her further to starboard when IT slid onto the transom. Or when IT smashed the outrigger. ITs head was so heavy. I couldn't stop myself falling towards IT. And ITs teeth, ITs . . .*

Christos tried to stop remembering but ITs image filled his mind. So close. IT wouldn't go away. He knew tiger sharks didn't eat for days or weeks and then gorged themselves on bait, or a dead whale if they were really lucky. They'd stalk a sick whale calf for days just waiting, waiting for it to die. Like this shark would wait now for him.

*Think about something else, Chris. Anything. Li'l Bit isn't holed that I can see, but I can't see right to the stern. She hasn't floated free so she must still be caught somewhere on the port side as well. Maybe she's holed on that side? The water . . .* He couldn't think about the water or what he would do if she was leaking.

*What will Dad say if she ... ? Who cares! He's not here. I am. I have to deal with it. But it's all right. She's not holed. I just have to wait. That's the plan. Wait. I'm going to be all right.*

He took a deep breath. His ribs hurt but he lifted himself on one elbow, then rolled so he could raise himself up onto his hands and knees. He stretched his neck carefully. The muscles in his back screamed.

*I must have hit the deck when Li'l Bit smashed into the bommie and again when IT dragged me out.* His stomach clenched.

*Don't think about it! If Dad was here he'd be yelling at me to get on with it. Even if I am just waiting there must be something else to do. Get yourself doing it!* Christos let his head loll around a few times in a circular motion. He felt his back with his hand, but pulled it away quickly when he touched the sore part. He groaned.

*I'll be covered in bruises tomorrow. Tomorrow, that's a good thought. The sun'll come up and it'll be tomorrow if I can just wait that long.* Now he was kneeling, his head throbbing with pain, his throat aching for water.

*You should have at least brought your water bottle. Nothing to eat on board either unless you like raw fish.* He rolled himself onto his back, stopping momentarily when a muscle spasmed.

*Feels like I've been hit by an oil tanker.*

His mother always said that what doesn't kill you makes you stronger.

*Great, I must nearly be Superman by now! It's better, though, when I think about Mum.* He remembered her gift, his fingers feeling for the chain around his neck. Saint Christopher. Patron saint of journeys and the lost.

*How did you know I'd need him, Mum?* But his fingers touched only bare skin. He felt all around his neck, over his shoulders, but it was gone. He'd lost it! His talisman, his present to keep him safe. He searched with scrabbling fingers around the floor.

*It must have fallen off when IT took me down. I'm sorry, Mum. You said you dreamed about my journey. What did you dream? That you'd never see me alive again?* Self-pity threatened to drown him.

*Get a grip on yourself, mate! You have to face facts. You're alone and no one is going to help. No one will miss you before tomorrow night and all of this will be over then, for good or ill. No one is going to save you.* Christos stared around. He could feel a lump in his throat and the warmth of tears he couldn't control.

*I didn't mean to lose it, Mum! I didn't mean for any of this to happen!* Christos moaned, his head hanging down on his knees, sobbing hopelessly.

Then he heard his father's voice.

'No good *blubbering. It won't make anything better. You have to do something. You'll never know, son, if you don't have a go.*'

'I am doing something!' Christos spoke to the empty boat. 'I'm waiting. I'm doing what I have to do.' But his father was right, he was a fool to cry. He wiped his eyes and cheeks with both his palms.

*It's these hands that are going to get me home safe tomorrow* . . . but Christos stopped himself.

Suddenly tomorrow offered no hope either. He had to deal with right now ... and then the moment after that – one moment after another, until this was over.

*From now on there is no tomorrow.*

He stared at the cut across his palm. It was deep and oozing blood. Now that he noticed it, it hurt too.

*Can't remember how I did that. Perhaps it was when IT bit the fish. I was close enough to smell ITs breath. Must have sliced my hand on ITs teeth. I was that close.* Christos began to shake uncontrollably as the memory took hold.

*Stop thinking about it or you'll go mad! Do something. Start the motor. You need to keep warm. But I can't crank her up without going out on deck again. I can't do it, not now, not after ... I'd rather die of cold. Well, maybe there's room to crawl up beside the motor and start it from inside? At least I'll be doing something.* He decided to try but, as he turned to find the torch, Christos saw water shining in its beam. He stared at it as though he was in a blinking game with one of his brothers.

First to blink loses. He blinked and it was still there, only a metre and a half from his feet.

*But when I crawled down there before there was no water. Li'l Bit doesn't have a hole in her. There shouldn't be any water. There isn't any water!* He refused to believe it – refused. *If I close my eyes it'll disappear.*

Christos opened his eyes again. The water was a fact. But a fact he couldn't face.

*If it was morning, if the sun was out I'd be all right. I'm just supposed to wait. That's what's supposed to happen.* But he knew now in his heart that the waiting plan was dead – he couldn't wait any longer. Water sloshed into the hull like waves across the beach on the incoming tide.

*You need to know where the water's coming from. Your life depends on knowing. Knowing and planning some way out.*

*But last time the plan didn't work. I almost died.*

*Something worked, you're still alive, aren't you!*

*But I stuffed it up. What if I stuff up again? What if I can't. If I'm too small.*

*You have no choice!*

*All right! But take it easy. Slowly. She's leaking, but how much? How long have we got?* Christos reached around until he found the bucket. Grabbing the filleting knife he crawled down the hull, stabbing the point into *Li'l Bit*'s keel to mark the water's edge.

*Now we wait. If I had my watch I could time it.*

*What difference will timing it make? If we're sinking, we're sinking and we won't make it through the night.*

*We might.* Christos knew they wouldn't, but despite himself he leaned back into the point of the bow and started to count.

'One potato, two potato . . .' But he lost count in the eighties.

*It's no good.* He kept glancing at his knife. He closed his eyes so he couldn't see it, but then in his imagination he saw the surface of dark waves under the torch beam and a fin slicing open the water's skin.

*It's worse now. I made it worse. I didn't need to put the fish in the icebox. It could have stayed in the kill-pit. I only wanted it so I could show off. That's why I went out there. It's my fault.* He wanted to scream but instead, from somewhere deep inside him, a voice started to sing.

'*Happy birthday to you,*
*Happy birthday to you,*
*Happy birthday, dear Christos,*
*Happy birthday to you.*'

His mother's voice, singing a childhood full of happy memories. On and on her voice sang and Christos mumbled along with her. 'Twinkle, twinkle little star', 'Waltzing Matilda', even the national anthem. His breathing steadied. He opened his eyes.

There was no mistake. The point of the knife was half a centimetre deep in water. He stared at it.

*Li'l Bit's sinking, and fast.* Christos felt as raw as freshly sliced steak.

*Falling overboard was just a bit of fun compared with waiting like this.* Now that he was aware of it, all Christos could hear was the sound of sloshing water. He made a noise deep in his chest. A type of moan that he repeated again and again, trying to drown out the sound of *Li'l Bit* drowning. Everything was different now.

*What'll I do? What will Dad say if I sink the dory? It's my fault. She was all right before my stupid plan.* If Li'l Bit *drowns at least they'll drag her up from the depths. If I'm lucky I'll drown first, before IT* . . . He cowered.

*I am going to die. Unless I can stop her sinking I am going to die.* Christos clutched like a drowning man at the hope he might be able to save *Li'l Bit.*

*I need to know where the water's coming from.* He grabbed the torch and stood up, ignoring the pain that stabbed through his body. He wrenched off the hatch cover, throwing it down onto the deck. Lifting the torch out into the darkness Christos swore, 'Stuff you!' The torch beam cut ten metres into the darkness before it was overcome by the heavy fog that roiled like steam from a crab cooker, white in the torchlight. He could see dark water surrounding the boat and then nothing but suffocating fog.

*Li'l Bit's* decks were wet, running water into the kill-pit. Christos felt like a gutted fish.

*I should have expected this. I know the fog comes three times, Dad always says so.*

Christos wrested his gaze away from the fog to the stern of the dory. *Li'l Bit* lay with the starboard side of her transom completely under water. IT had pulled her down even deeper than before. She was held fast in the coral's claws. The incoming tide rose relentlessly, wave by wave, like evening shadows lengthening, their fingers inching ever closer. Even as he watched, a swell lifted the hatch cover from the standing-pit and poured more than a bucketful of water into the hull.

*Another wave like that and the cover will lift off completely, then there'll be nothing to stop the sea from pouring in. Nothing to stop the sea from taking her . . . and me. Maybe I can bail her out? I've got a bucket.* A large swell poured into the hull. *Who am I kidding. I can't keep up with the tide.*

*Li'l Bit's sinking and now I know why. If we sit here like this the sea will just keep coming. So much for her popping up as the tide lifts around her. IT's taken care of that. She'll be full of water and completely without buoyancy soon. What'll I do?* He'd clutched at straws and failed.

# CHAPTER 10

His mind was numb and grey as the fog, but ideas still cut through its shadows like lightning through storm clouds.

*There must be a way. Maybe I could throw one of the fish from the icebox over the stern? Once I knew IT was eating that I could dive off Li'l Bit's bow and swim to safety?*

It was an idea, but Christos knew he wouldn't get back in the water. He couldn't begin to imagine what it would be like swimming near-naked through the black sea, his body stretched out horizontal and vulnerable, waiting to feel the serrated edges of ITs teeth tear at his stomach – wondering when. His skin turned to gooseflesh.

*Stop thinking about it, Chris.*

Suddenly the sea beside the dory exploded. The air alive with spray. Christos ducked below deck. Garfish flew like shrapnel, some shooting into the kill-pit. From safe inside he could hear the dying fish flip-flopping on the kill-pit floor. He listened until the flipping stopped, willing just one to reach the water. But their choice had only ever been about how to die. At least now they would never feel a shark's teeth.

Christos knew what had happened. The gar were attracted to the torchlight. IT had herded them between the coral and *Li'l Bit*'s hull until IT was too close to them and they panicked, exploding in an eruption of water. IT probably hadn't even meant to herd them, IT was simply looking. ITs curiosity had been rewarded before.

Christos could almost see IT watching, ITs tail sweeping languorously from side to side like a slow windscreen wiper, ready at any moment to burst into a frenzied attack.

*You have to do something, Chris. Maybe I can rock the dory? It's worth a try.* Christos rolled around until his shoulders were against one side of the hull, then, bracing his feet against her ribs on the other side, he threw his weight backwards and forwards.

'Come on!' he grunted. 'Move!' *Li'l Bit* didn't budge. He kept at it, side to side, but she was jammed solid. Christos slumped down, panting, across the keel. The water was a quarter of the way up the blade of his filleting knife. He could hear it now, pouring in through the standing-pit hatch like water over a dam slipway, menacing and heavy.

*Maybe I should throw both the fish over the side? It's not such a bad idea. If IT's fed well enough IT won't be interested in me. I'll just breaststroke away silently into the night.* But the same flaw spoiled that idea as spoiled his first one.

*I won't be swimming anywhere.*

*But maybe if Li'l Bit does go under she won't be*

*completely covered?* It was a worthless hope. From the bottom of the low to the top of the high, the tide was almost four and a half metres. If *Li'l Bit* stayed stuck where she was the tide would cover her completely. The picture flashed into his mind of him teetering on tiptoe on the point of her bow, trying to keep his head above the surface. A fin slashing through the ocean beside him, feeling for his dark-blooded heartbeat in the dead water.

'I can't do this anymore.' For a moment

Christos slipped beneath the surface, his courage failed. Drawing his knees up to his chest he sat staring blindly ahead.

'I wish I was already dead, *Li'l Bit*.' He'd never seen a dead person. Animals, yes, fish – but a person, never.

Christos closed his eyes. His mind filled with a scene of dead bodies from a documentary he saw once about World War One. All those young soldiers floundering like stranded fish in a fog of mustard gas. The dying falling on the dead.

*That's how I feel. They died because they couldn't stop breathing. They died because they never stopped wanting to stay alive.*

Then it struck him.

*IT wants to stay alive too. IT wants to eat. Why don't I use ITs hunger against IT? What if I go fishing, but this time for the shark? What if I use my fish as bait to catch IT? If IT's strong enough to jam Li'l Bit into the coral then surely IT's strong enough to pull her out into the channel again?*

Suddenly hope shone like a torch beam in the darkness.

*Maybe it will work. Maybe if I rig a fishing line?* But he dismissed the idea immediately. He'd seen what the shark did to his two other lines. Snapped them like cotton.

'What if I double the line cord, Li'l Bit?' Christos asked. *Make it stronger. No, it still won't be enough. Maybe I just use the trace? No, it might break and I've only got one chance.* Christos furrowed his brow, thinking hard.

*That's it! The anchor rope! I could use it. It's four times as thick as the line cord, or thicker!* His hands trembled as he pulled the rope towards him.

*I'll tie the rope to the Samson post, that's the strongest part of* Li'l Bit. *Then I'll tie the bait to the other end and throw it out over the stern. If I can keep the line pulling straight backwards IT should pull us out into the deeper water every time it attacks the fish.* Christos clambered up and squatted on the keel.

*It'll be dangerous. IT'll pull the bow up and sink the stern to begin with, but only till she's free.*

'That's it, *Li'l Bit*. I'll get us out of this.' Christos trembled with relief and apprehension.

*First, get the fish out of the icebox.* The thought of going out on deck slowed his enthusiasm.

*Then I won't go on deck. I'll crawl up beside the motor, open the engine hatch, reach over and lift the lid on the icebox. That way I don't have to go out there. I can do it now!*

Christos grabbed the torch and pulled the knife out of the keel, reaching for his forgotten shorts. He half-stood in the cramped space so he could slip them on.

*Now I'm ready.* It seemed strange but he felt stronger, more confident, being dressed.

*I can do this.*

'If IT comes looking for me IT'll get this in the eye,' he threatened, brandishing the knife for *Li'l Bit* to see, pumping himself full of bravado.

*I'll have to hurry or the water'll be too deep beside the motor.* He crouched down and half-crawled in under the deck. The water came close to halfway up his thighs. It was warmer than he expected too – or he was colder than he remembered. He squeezed in beside the motor and pushed himself upwards, sliding awkwardly against the uneven metal edges.

*Lucky the motor's cold. Wouldn't be doing this if it was hot. Maybe my luck's changing?*

Christos pushed upwards until the back of his bowed head touched the bottom of the hatch cover. Paused. Sweat trickled on his neck. He tried to concentrate.

*What's the plan? You just have to lean out, open the hatch cover and drag out the biggest fish. At no time will you be out on deck. You're safe. This bit of the plan's completely safe. If IT appears, just duck back into the engine hatch, quick. Now, on the count of three.*

*One . . .*

*Two . . .*

*Three!*

The engine hatch cover flew upwards. Christos bounced out like a jack-in-the-box, throwing himself towards the icebox. The torch beam skidded crazily for a moment then focused on the icebox lid. Christos did not look towards the sea. He worked like a robot.

*Balance the torch on the lip of the engine hatch. Icebox lid up. Grab fish by tail. Drag fish out. Close icebox lid. Drag fish over to engine hatch. Push fish down head first beside motor. Grab torch.*

Only when the job was done did Christos allow himself to glance towards the stern. The water was almost to the level of the standing-pit. Soon the sea would simply pour into *Li'l Bit.*

Then IT appeared again, close behind the dory. IT cruised past, ITs gliding bulk darkening the tenebrous sea.

Christos sank beneath the lid of the engine hatch, pulling it closed to cover him.

*IT knows me! IT knows everything I think. IT knew my plan before I started. IT knows IT'll have the meat off my bones. It's only a matter of time.*

His stomach clenched into its familiar knot. He felt the water close above him as IT dragged him helplessly down into the darkness.

'I'm fooling myself, *Li'l Bit*. Maybe I should just do it, just jump into the water now and get it over with. How long will it take? A minute, two before IT finds me? A few seconds of pain and I won't feel anything ever again.'

It was his mother who stopped him, just like she did when he was a kid having a bad nightmare.

'*It's all right, Christos. I'm here now. Nothing's going to hurt you.*' And he believed her now because he wanted to believe he would live, more than he had ever wanted anything in his entire life. He leaned against the cold metal of the motor.

'I'm all right. I'm all right,' he kept muttering, his eyes clenched shut, his whole body shivering hard.

*I've done the first part of my plan and I did that right. I've got the fish. I have to finish it. There are no choices left.*

Christos lay as though dead, draped over the cold motor, unable to force his body to move. Perhaps he was there for a long time, he couldn't tell. It was the sound of water pouring into the hull that roused him once more. Now every ripple was enough to slop another litre or two into *Li'l Bit*. Every swell sloshed bucketfuls more. Christos raised his head.

*Do it!*

Still grasping the fish's tail in his hand, he slipped to his knees beside the motor. The water was deep enough to wet his shorts but at least it made dragging the fish back to the front of the dory easier.

Christos laid the mackerel along the keel. Already its head was in water. He unshackled the anchor rope from the chain. But when he held it in his hands he knew he hadn't thought this through.

*IT'll hit the fish hard the first time but once it shakes ITs head a few times IT'll cut straight through the rope. If one strike isn't enough to pull Li'l Bit free, then the whole plan fails. IT has to drag on that fish for as long as I can make it.* He knew he'd have to use something else.

'You fool! The anchor chain!' Christos yelled, startling himself in the enclosed space.

'That's it, fish,' he said, shaking it by the tail. 'I'll wrap you in the anchor chain. IT'll never cut that!' The idea energised him. His hands began working feverishly. He reshackled the anchor rope to the chain, tightening it with the pliers. Then he unshackled the anchor from the other end. Christos stuffed the shackle-end through the fish's mouth so the chain extended down one side of it, through its mouth, then back up the other side. He wrapped both ends of the chain around its tail, then shackled them together. He could hear water dribbling continuously now, when

143

it wasn't pouring in at the top of the swell. Water was under his feet.

*Hurry!*

The fish lay between the lengths of chain like filling in a sandwich. Christos stabbed the filleting knife repeatedly through the fish until five gaping wounds pierced its flesh. Gouging out both its eyes he cut lengths of trace wire, threading them through the chain links on one side, through the eye sockets and wounds, then through the chain links on the other side. He tied both sides together over the top of the fish, then again underneath. When he'd finished, the fish lay trussed like a Christmas turkey.

*The bait's ready. What's next? The line. If there's ten metres of chain, less about two metres around the fish, then I've got eight metres left. Li'l Bit's just over five metres long so add five more metres of rope. That'll keep IT well behind the stern.*

The chain was heavy and he hoped all the action would happen well beneath the surface.

*Keep IT as far away from me as possible! If*

*this doesn't work, if IT pulls too hard from port or starboard rather than from astern, Li'l Bit will capsize, and then . . . ? The plan will work! Don't listen to the water.*

Christos measured three double armlengths of rope, coiling it, and the chain, beside the fish.

*Now I have to tie off the anchor rope.* He'd never fished for sharks before but he knew the Samson post was the only part of *Li'l Bit* strong enough to take the force IT would unleash. That meant putting his body out onto the foredeck to tie the rope off there. All he could hear was the thump of his heart inside his ears. He tried to think about something else. The look on her face when she saw him again. But his imagination wouldn't co-operate the closer he came to the plan's end.

*Okay then, all I have to do is open the top edge of the hatch, put my hands out and throw a couple of figure eights round the Samson post. Don't have to leave the hatch. I could do it in the dark.* Christos didn't wait for his doubts to make a coward of him. He pushed the hatch cover up and back until it was halfway open.

*That's enough. Now.*

His hands snaked out of the hatch.

*It's only thirty centimetres.* Christos felt for the T-piece. He threw three figure eights, then a hitch around the bottom, pulling it as tight as he could before slipping the hatch cover back into place. When he was finished his hands shook uncontrollably.

*It's done. It's done. I've done it.*

Christos sat down on the keel in his spot between the coils of anchor rope. It was strange how familiar beneath the deck had become in a few short hours.

*It's almost like my bedroom. I know every coil of rope and link of chain, every one of Li'l Bit's ribs and the . . . lifejacket. Chris, what are you thinking? Get the bloody thing on now, you fool.*

'I can't believe I haven't. I'm an idiot. Idiot!'

Untying the knot was simple in the torch-light. It was an old jacket that looked like a baby's bib stuffed front and back with pillows. As he pulled it down over his head and tied the tape tight around his waist, Christos felt secure, invincible, like a knight strapped into his armour. But the feeling was short-lived.

*I'm ready! Now for the last throw of the dice. It's fishing time.*

Christos rubbed his right thumb hard against the palm of his left hand. The movement steadied the shaking. He could hear his father's voice.

'So this is how you plan things, is it, Chris? You still have to get the bait out over the stern. That's at the other end of the dory. You can't go under the deck because it's full of water. That means you go back out there or we sink. And you have to go right down to the stern, because you can't throw the bait that far, can you? It's too heavy.' Christos knew his father was right; just another thing he'd refused to think about.

*There's no alternative. IT's only a shark, Chris. You've seen hundreds of them.* He tried to convince himself. But everything really had changed since he'd gone overboard. Everything. He'd skipped over the one small flaw in his plan. Once more he saw ITs eye, threw the fish at IT, unable to untangle his leg, down in the deadwater darkness. Christos lost balance, throwing out a hand to stop himself falling.

'I can't! Mum! Dad! No! I can't!' He clawed at the air around him like a drowning swimmer. To go out again into the jaws of that nightmare was too much to ask. Too much.

*I have a plan! Everything is in the plan! Stuff it up this time, Chris, and you're dead!* His mind reeled. He grabbed at his legs, clutching them to his chest, rocking forward and back. But he toppled to the side instead, his face hitting the keel hard. His lips moved but no sound came. He lay still for a long time, eyes clamped shut, seeing nothing, hearing nothing, until something touched his hair. Delicately, like the soft touch of fingers, water was wetting it.

*Like Mum touched my hair sometimes as she sat on my bed before I went to sleep. Make it go away,*

*Mum. Things were easy when I was a kid. Come and make it be all right, like you used to.* But his mother would not speak.

*Dad, where are you?* But his father too had fallen silent.

*It's night-time. I am alone. The water is coming and no one can do a thing, no one but me.*

*No, that's not true. Karis will know something's wrong, call out a search party. If she was here I could do anything. But I'm a coward alone. I can't face IT alone.* Christos sat up quickly. His hair dripping onto his chest. He could see the depth of the water flooding the hull.

*Any more and I won't be able to start the motor. There's always only me — now or never.*

Christos hoisted the anchor chain, dragging it and the fish into position under the hatch cover. He reached up and pushed the cover out of the way. It slid over the fog-wet deck, splashing into the sea.

*I've lost it! What'll I tell Dad? That—doesn't—matter.* Christos thought slowly now, as if his mind was stuck in mud.

*IT will hear.* But he was past caring. *Aren't I trying to catch IT anyway? I want IT to hear.*

He hoisted the fish above him, out onto the deck. It was heavier than anything he could remember. He let it go. The fish slipped down the wet deck towards the kill-pit before the chain caught on the for'ard hatch coaming.

*That's good. Maybe I can just push it into the water.* For one fantastic moment he nearly believed he could push the fish down the deck and over the stern without leaving safety.

*Don't be crazy. You know it'll end up in the kill-pit. Don't lie to yourself anymore, Chris.* He dragged hard on the chain, pulling the fish back up until its tail hung over the edge of the hatch above him. He grabbed it with both hands like an axe handle raised above his head. Aiming for the stern, he thrust the fish as hard as he could, torpedoing it across the wet deck. The chain clattered down, pulled by the fish's weight, falling after it like a handful of loose change, into the kill-pit.

*IT must have heard that. Good, IT'll come looking for me.*

Christos sank down on his haunches and closed his eyes. The empty sea waited, as he waited for his heart to stop. But it wouldn't, not this time.

*I know how it feels, my heart, like a live man encased in a coffin. Pounding so somebody will hear and let him out.* But then Christos heard the other sound. The sound of water flowing like a small waterfall into the dory. The sound that forced him on.

*This will work, Chris.*

*And if it doesn't?*

*I have to go. On the count of three.*

'One,' he whispered.

'Two,'

'Three!'

Christos did not move.

His heart, his stomach, empty. His legs warm and wet. Tears pouring.

'I can't! You can't make me!' He slumped down onto the anchor rope. His sobs shaking him until he calmed, whimpering.

'Please, someone. Please.' He knew now

how those soldiers in the trenches felt. Before they went over the top into the machine gun's mouth. Before they met IT. He had met IT and IT had shot him down, shot down his faith in his mind, his heart, his hands.

*Mum believes in God. Maybe God will help.* He tried to pray. Tried to clear his mind for the moment it would take to say the words, but his head flooded with images of soldiers bleeding and dying. He couldn't stop them, pictures of soldiers he could not help.

*It's no use, I can't pray. Dad, help, what do you believe in?*

*'People. That's what life's about. I've got you kids and your mother and . . . that's it. People to care about.'* It was the same answer he gave when Christos was the little kid who asked his father what love was.

'But I'm alone.'

*They did it, didn't they, those soldiers? They soiled their pants but they still went over the top. Yes they did, but their mates were there to keep them fixed to hope. To smoke their final smoke with. To* tell their one last joke to. To write their final letters home.

I'll write a letter too, then. A letter no one will ever read.

Dear Karis

At the going down of the sun and in the morning I will think of you. I've chosen you because I know that they won't mind, my family and friends. They know it's not wrong to care for someone special above all of them. They know I don't love them any less because of it.

I thought I could do this, you know. I thought I could do anything. I've done it all a hundred times before. But Dad was always with me then. It's all changed now. He told Mum I could do this trip by myself. Maybe he was wrong?

It's strange, isn't it, talking to you like this when you hardly even know I exist? Or do you? I like to think, actually right now I need to think, that you think about me too.

Christos took a breath, holding it in deep, picturing her face, the way she wore her hair.

> *Karis, thank you. You're here when I need you to keep my courage straight. But I've never felt like this before. I'm so frightened I can't make my body do what it has to. I must keep hope. I must have faith. I must believe in you.*
>
> *If you were here I'd be calm. I'd want to show off, to hug you, to laugh with you, to smell your hair, and I would die to save you. But before I died I'd want you to know this – if the way I feel about you is what love is, then this, and only this, is to die for.*
>
> *You give me the strength to do what I have to.*
> *With all my love,*
> *Chris*

154

He took the torch, raising himself on uncertain legs until he stood, holding to the edges of the hatch. His body shook. Fresh warmth dribbled down one thigh. But he had conquered his mind. Christos leaned forward until he tipped onto his belly, then slipped down the wet deck, following the fish into the kill-pit.

# CHAPTER 11

The fog coiled in black billows around the boat, swallowing the light. Christos stood in the kill-pit flicking the torch beam around *Li'l Bit*'s stern. Nothing. Only the dark ocean. Only silence. The water rose and fell in a breathing swell. He watched the waves pour into the standing-pit with each breath.

Christos could hear his heart's red gush. He fought to control his hands, grabbing at the edge of the deck. It was hard to balance in the kill-pit, his legs almost refusing to work. But his mind was clear. Christos forced himself, and with every movement won the battle. He put the torch down on the upper side of the engine hatch.

*Quick. Do this quickly. Don't turn your back to the sea.* The fish lay on the low starboard side of the kill-pit floor.

*Too close to the sea for comfort.* He steadied himself.

*What next?*

Christos sat on the port side as far from the stern as he could. Grabbing the chain, he hauled the fish up. Bracing his feet against the edge of the kill-pit to stop himself slipping down, he dragged hard on the chain.

*When I've finished it'll be done, for better or for worse.*

When IT appeared he held the fish cradled in his arms. IT cruised into the circle of light, out of the deep water. He froze, but his heart was crashing in hurricane waves. His mouth fell open. IT came closer, closer, slowly, languorously, right on the surface. Gunmetal-grey and striped. The tiger. Christos did not blink. He did nothing. Thought nothing. Watched. IT cruised to the stern. He saw ITs eye turned up to him, assessing, almost tasting. Then IT veered away like a jet fighter banking off into a black-liquid sky. ITs grey side took so long to pass. Then he breathed again.

*Don't think, act! Quick, while IT's turning.*

Holding the fish before him, Christos clambered back to the high side of the stern. Now the fish hardly seemed heavy at all. He swung it backwards then threw it overboard. The chain slithered after it as though he'd dropped the anchor. Christos paused for a moment.

*That's that. Now IT has to help me. Please.* He turned to get back to safety, but too late. *Li'l Bit* jerked backwards as the chain wrenched taut.

IT bit like a savage dog, snapping at the bait, then sawing side to side to cut the fish. Christos fell on his back in the kill-pit. Threw his legs out to brace himself against the sides. The chain ground along the gunwale. IT thrashed to cut the fish, but couldn't. Suddenly the chain whipped across the stern, fell the length of the transom and dropped off the starboard side.

'Not that way!' Christos screamed. 'It'll drown us that way!' The transom plunged down into the ocean as *Li'l Bit*'s bow lurched upward, rearing like a frightened horse. IT was dragging her down. Christos clutched at the deck but couldn't get a hold. The chain smashed against the torch. Its beam slashed wildly as it flew over the side, plunging *Li'l Bit* into foggy twilight. He pushed back hard with his legs, crawling up the side of the kill-pit, trying to stop himself from following the torch as *Li'l Bit* reared again.

Christos felt the huge weight of water heft inside *Li'l Bit*'s hull, moving in one heavy wave, forcing her down. The standing-pit was underwater, filling like an open storm drain. *Li'l Bit* lifted further onto her starboard side.

*She's going to roll!* Christos threw himself flat on his face, trying to hold himself in the kill-pit. A huge crack sounded from under the starboard hull. Water gushed beneath him, sea pouring freely into the dory. The wave inside *Li'l Bit* kicked back to the other side and she groaned, still not free. Her stern was down worse than before. Sinking.

*I failed.*

*We'll die!*

The anchor chain lay above him. Christos rolled, clutching at it to steady himself. He pulled it down. The chain fell slack in his hand.

*IT's let go! If IT's ripped the bait free IT won't be back.* Li'l Bit's *drowning. No! Please! Help me!*

Christos scrambled up; clutching the chain in one hand, praying there was still bait on the end.

*Get the chain topside. If IT comes back the line has to be in place. And keep it there!* He threw himself into the water that covered the line tray, forgetting everything but pushing the chain up, up until it was back over the high port side.

The sea erupted behind the dory. Dumping bucketfuls of water on him.

*The bait's still on the line! Li'l Bit* pulled back again but this time he could feel her take the strain from the opposite direction.

*Keep the chain up!*

IT was pulling where he wanted. In fog and utter darkness, he could hear IT. IT must have come from underneath, forcing the bait to the surface, forcing the fish back into ITs jaws.

*This . . . must . . . work!* Christos rolled into the kill-pit, his legs braced against the bottom side, holding the chain over his shoulders. It cut down, shuddering with vibrations as IT rolled.

*MUST!*

IT thundered in waves of shattered sea behind *Li'l Bit*, pulling like a dog enraged at the chain. *Li'l Bit* rolled back, stern still in the water.

But the pull was different now. IT was not attacking. IT was rolling fast, spraying him with water, and then IT dived.

*Something's happened.* The weight fell from his back as the chain jumped along the side of the gunwale towards the bow. The chain was jerking downwards now and out towards the open sea. *Li'l Bit* lifted.

*She felt it too.* The water shifted in her again. Christos thought he felt her move. Then, as though in slow motion, she *was* moving! Rolling back, back to port. The coral grinding beneath her. Rolling to port then righting herself slowly, pregnant with water. Heavy with sea she turned, obedient to the dragging chain. IT heaved her, bow down, away from the reef.

Christos couldn't think. Didn't know how it happened. But they were free.

*Thank you! Thank you!* The chain links knotted as IT rolled, he could hear them crunch together. The torch floated, still shining, near the reef. But even as he watched, the fog closed over it. As the distance widened he could only make out a faint glow, then all light was gone.

IT rolled again, thrashing and dragging. Back up on the surface now, the splashes so huge he could almost feel the weight of the water. *Li'l Bit*'s bow dipped almost to the sea's surface, raising her stern. The water inside her rushed forward.

Christos didn't know how, but he was certain they'd caught the shark and now *Li'l Bit* was shackled to IT.

*That cracking sound? What if she's holed? I'm further from shore than before. Have to get to land.*

'Let go!' he screamed at IT. 'She's free! Let us go!'

Christos rolled over, threw open the engine cover and dragged himself to his knees in front of it. He had to try and drown IT. Drag IT backwards. He flicked the decompression lever up, grabbed the handle.

'Please!' One, two … He grunted with the effort, dropping the valve. *Li'l Bit* didn't let him down. She fired, spluttering at first, then idling steady. IT thrashed the sea, still dragging him further from land. *Li'l Bit* bucked. ITs every wrench threw a wave through the water inside her causing her to nod dangerously backwards and forwards, end to end.

*If IT pulls to either side with this much water in her she has to roll. Just when things are getting better, they go to hell.* He had to get to land.

*Li'l Bit* bucked and dipped, the swell complicating the way she pitched.

*Maybe I can cut the anchor rope? But I'll have*

*to go for'ard. What if I end up in the drink again with IT?* Lifejacket or not, he couldn't do it.

Balancing on the crazed deck, he crawled to the standing-pit.

*Get her to land!* Slipping in, he kicked *Li'l Bit* into reverse. The propeller cavitated in too little water but he jammed the throttle down hard. As she rocked backwards, the prop bit. *Li'l Bit* groaned at the bow, churning foam at the stern. He could feel IT fighting, but he could feel IT weakening, ITs power ebbing with each thrash of ITs massive frame.

*Keep going backwards. That'll keep IT fighting straight on to the bow. IT won't be able to pull from the side and, if I go fast enough, IT'll drown.* The thought of being rid of IT spurred him on.

*I need to counteract the weight of the water up front.* Christos ducked into the standing-pit, feeling around for the fuel drum. Unhooking its jockey strap, he heaved it out into the line tray, shifting that much weight as far as he could to the rear. Then he ducked down again to hook the tiller on a hard lock to starboard.

*I'll drive an arc backwards around the reef and straight into land. It'll take time, but we'll get there.*

Jamming his feet under the standing-pit deck he sat in the line tray and leaned back, putting all his weight as far to stern as he could. Hanging out over the black sea. *Li'l Bit* gained some traction. He could feel her prop biting, could hear the motor under a more constant strain. He felt her move backwards, but only just. She was a quarter full of water and dragging ITs full weight as IT fought against her – but *Li'l Bit* was making way.

# CHAPTER 12

Christos heard a final splash in the fog off *Li'l Bit*'s bow before IT fought no more. When IT was fighting the whole boat had shuddered but now there was only ITs dead weight dragging, a constant pressure on the anchor rope.

*IT's dead.*

'Thank you, Karis,' he whispered in that moment's peace. But the old fear quickly returned. *Li'l Bit* might still be sinking.

*If she is holed she might be self-draining, the water sucking out of her like a loose paper from the window of a moving car. Or I might be forcing more water into her like a car without a windscreen, if the hole's too big. Damned if I do, damned if I don't! Either way we have to get to land quickly, and if we have to get somewhere quickly we go forwards.*

He knocked down the revs, kicked the gearbox into neutral and unhooked the tiller. As soon as he felt the prop stop he kicked the gearbox back into gear and *Li'l Bit* leaned forward. Christos knocked up the revs, but before he could give *Li'l Bit* her head the anchor rope swung back quickly. The dory had caught up with the shark. He knew IT was still there, so close, but hidden under the vast night fog. He couldn't see IT but he could feel ITs weight as the chain slipped along the gunwale. He steered carefully to avoid fouling it around the propeller. He stared ahead as IT passed, muttering an incantation against his terror.

'IT's dead. IT's dead. IT's dead.'

But he couldn't be calm, even after he felt the chain slide down the length of the gunwale and knew that IT was no longer gliding through the deadwater beside him. Even after he arranged the chain to pull straight from the Samson post over the centre of the stern. After he gave *Li'l Bit* the gun and the motor groaned, lifting her bow to drag ITs dead weight behind her. Even then he couldn't be calm, knowing IT was out there behind him. He thought again of jettisoning IT but dismissed the idea.

*If* Li'l Bit *is sinking there isn't time. IT's dead. We killed IT, and IT's dead.* Slowly and deliberately, Christos turned his back on the sea, peering forward to steer the dory through the blinding fog.

The water inside flowed back from the bow to weigh down the stern even more, washing against his calves as *Li'l Bit* made way. He heaved the fuel drum out of the line tray and back into the kill-pit.

*Should put it right up front, but can't waste time. The motor must be standing in water already.* Half of the transom had disappeared under the surface, more when *Li'l Bit* drove through a swell. He was almost sitting on the sea's skin, so close to its darkness, but he didn't flinch.

*IT is dead. Concentrate on avoiding the reef and getting the beach lined up. But where is the reef, or the island? Where am I?* He saw nothing but grey fog and the pale deck.

*What if I hit another bommie?* Christos was shivering again, if he'd ever stopped.

Then out of the darkness, faint as a candle at first then growing to a dull glow, the torch appeared, bobbing in the trackless sea. As though it was waiting for them. Christos would have mustered a smile if he'd had the energy to do so.

'I knew we'd get there, *Li'l Bit!*' He patted the deck repeatedly. He knew the torch had fallen into the channel, so with the tide coming in it should be closer to shore, away from the reef. Just to be safe, though, he veered further to starboard, knocked back the revs and came up on the southern side of the torch – backing his judgement that it had floated the way he guessed. For a moment though, he was uncertain. The old panic rising. But everything was different now.

'I'll get the torch,' he heard himself say. 'I need it and it's there.' His voice was calm. 'I'll get the torch. I'll motor past, lean over with the landing net and scoop it up. Might miss it with the gaff.' His father would call him an amateur for using the net. 'Say what you like, Dad. I can live with it.'

Christos pulled out the long-handled net. *Li'l Bit* was close enough for him to see the torch bobbing like a lighthouse on the sea's surface. Five metres, four metres, three … He leaned slightly to port, not too far or he'd unbalance the water inside the hull. He steadied his hands on the handle and scooped the torch up, his foot already steering *Li'l Bit* away to starboard. Christos caught a glimpse of the coral, the rocks, even the bulk of the sleeping cod. The bommie was off to port, right where he thought it should be. He saw again the beauty of the garden and remembered it for the gift it was.

*When I remember this day it'll be for the beauty too, not only for the terror.*

He stowed the net. Grasping the torch in both his hands, Christos held it above his head, directing the beam as far forward as he could. He gave *Li'l Bit* her head.

*If I go slowly in the shallow water, the shark might catch on the bottom. Besides, she could still be sinking.* He had forgotten about that for a few blessed minutes. Then the bottom turned to white sand, reflecting the torchlight.

*We're close now. Just a bit more. Just a little bit . . .* Christos kicked the dory out of gear. *Li'l Bit* rode a small wave in. He could feel the shark bumping across the sandy bottom but even IT couldn't hold her back now. She rode that final swell as sweet as a seabird until her keel kissed the sand.

Christos waited for the wash to catch up before he jumped forward, switching off the fuel to the motor. It died almost before he'd closed the hatch. The water inside the hull rocked backwards and forwards, threatening to roll *Li'l Bit* on her side. But it was over now. The sea rose and fell between the rocks. He could hear it and smell the salt and taste it too. It tasted good.

Christos walked unsteadily for'ard, pulled up the anchor from the hatch and threw it out onto the beach. Then he jumped down onto the sand. His knees almost gave beneath him. He leaned, shivering, against *Li'l Bit*'s bow, more tired than he could ever remember. He could hardly lift his arms to drag the anchor rope out of the hold, tie it off on the eye bolt and tie the looped end to the anchor. He buried it above the flotsam of highwater.

'You'll be safe till morning,' he said. 'Wait for me.' The tide might leave her high and dry or she might sink, but he couldn't think about any of that now.

*Now I need to sleep.* The torch beam picked out his earlier tracks and he followed them slowly to his camp.

The lifejacket was almost too much, but Christos got the knots undone. He slid down into his sleeping bag until it covered his head. It was wet with fog and full of sand now from his feet, but he didn't care. He reached out and pulled the lifejacket to him for a pillow.

Christos switched off the torch, closed his eyes and, within seconds, he slept a sleep without dreams.

174

# CHAPTER 13

When he woke it was daylight, grey daylight shrouded in fog, but still lit by real sun.

*Morning!* The morning he thought he might never live to see. He smiled. It hurt his face, but smiling was good; hurting was good too.

*Li'l Bit!*

Christos tried to sit but doubled over in pain, rolling onto the pile of unlit firewood beside him. Every part of his body ached. His head too. He was thirsty and his stomach groaned.

Li'l Bit *will have to wait.*

He dragged himself from his sleeping bag, wincing as he tried to stretch his muscles. Standing on uneasy legs, he leaned back on the casuarina for balance. Christos unhooked his food bag and took out the water bottle, tipping it up until he had to breathe, then drinking deeply once more. His stomach churned. Suddenly he felt ravenous too. He dived back into his food bag for the remaining bread and salami, tearing at it like a shark. He swallowed fast, washing it down until he felt almost human again. He leaned against the she-oak.

*Now, let's see about* Li'l Bit, *and about going home.*

Christos rubbed his head and tried to flatten the bird's nest of his hair. He glanced uncertainly towards the beach.

*I'll pack up camp first then I won't have to come back again.* He was reluctant to leave. The night's events kept playing over again and again in his mind.

*In camp there's nothing to be frightened of. Last night all seems unreal here. Not so sure how I'll feel out on the beach, or at sea. Still, you'll never know if you don't have a go.* He smiled.

Christos slapped the sand out of his sleeping bag and rolled it up, stowing it in the food bag along with his torch, the lifejacket and the water bottle. His shirt was wet with fog but he put it on anyway.

*That's better, I feel dressed now.* His watch was still there too, hanging in the tree. It was just before five a.m. He slipped it onto his wrist. Christos heaved the bag onto his shoulder. Under his shirt his skin was red raw and tender where the chain had cut his back. He winced at more pain.

*When the sun comes out properly I'll check for bruises. I'll be covered in them for sure.*

Then he couldn't put it off any longer. He was ready to face what had to be faced, to do what had to be done.

Even through the fog Christos could see *Li'l Bit* from the top of the dune. The anchor had dragged straight down the beach, but she was there, floating in the outgoing tide, pulling back like a harnessed horse as she rode over a wave. As he walked down to her he could see the broken outrigger jutting from her side like a snapped toothpick and the black scars on her deck where the cleats had been ripped out.

*It wasn't a dream then, or even a nightmare. Last night was real.*

Christos felt a lump in his throat.

'I couldn't have done it without you, *Li'l Bit*,' he said to the dory. But then he stopped, feeling too … sentimental. 'Thanks,' he continued more matter-of-factly, 'for not letting me die.' Then he laughed aloud.

*I can't believe you're still floating. You look like a big, fat duck sitting that low in the water.* He smiled again, tasting the salt on his lips. *Let's go home.*

Relief flooded through him until he saw IT. The shark lolled in the small waves. Its head was thrust into the loop of anchor chain where the fish had been tied, like a condemned man's head in a hangman's noose. As IT rolled to free itself IT must have wound the noose tighter and tighter until IT drowned. Christos's gaze did not leave IT as he waded into the shallows to load his bag into the for'ard hatch. He jumped onto the deck and leaned in to pull up the bucket which he emptied into the transom tray before freeing the pliers from the rest of the clutter.

*I'll sort that mess out on the way home.*

The idea of home felt good, but Christos knew there was something he had to do before he could leave. Even though he knew, as IT lay dead in the light of day, that he was ITs master, Christos knew he had to make his peace. His gaze returned to the shark. As he jumped down into the water beside IT, fear prickled at the hairs on his neck.

But now he felt more awe at its defeated strength than fear. It was at least four and a half metres long and even in death he could feel its power. He forced himself to look at its head. A seagull had already found the carcass and feasted on its eye, the eye that had watched him all night, leaving a bloodied socket and a streak of white down its grey side. In the cold dawn light he felt nothing but pity, a profound sadness for his dead adversary, despite all the shark had cost him.

Now that he could look back on the night, catching the shark seemed like a cheap trick, a tragic game. He was sad it had died.

*I didn't mean for it to happen. It was a mistake. The whole night was a mistake. My fault and no one else's.*

He looked more closely at the carcass. Whole raw chunks had been ripped out of its underside, its guts spilled onto the clean sand.

*Only another shark could have done that.* Christos crouched down beside it.

*I hope you were dead when it attacked. You were fighting for your own life too, weren't you? Now I know what that feels like.*

'Don't be stupid, Chris. It's dead! None of this is getting you home. Get the anchor chain.' Christos smiled. He was talking sense. He gripped the pliers in his hand. The fish's head was still tied in the chain beside the shark's jaws. Reaching down he unscrewed the D shackle then cut the unbroken sprag wire ties that still held what was left of the carcass of the fish in place. Christos dragged and wriggled the shark with his foot to free the chain from around its red-bruised body, then carried the chain to the for'ard hatch and dumped it in.

*Sort that out later too. Now for* Li'l Bit.

He walked around the dory, running his hands down her sides where the paint was scraped off by the coral, marking her with black battle scars. But her plywood hull was still intact.

*Never holed, not ever!* Christos felt like kissing her.

*When we get home I'll paint you completely, and then I'm going to write your name across your transom. In black, outlined with gold:* Li'l Bit. He stopped himself. *It sounds stupid but I am going to, it's the least I can do.*

Christos climbed back aboard then and started to bail out the water. As he worked he imagined what he would say to them all, his parents, brothers and sisters, the fishermen, and her. The thought of Karis spurred him on. As he stood in the kill-pit fuelling *Li'l Bit* up for the journey home, his eye caught something lying on the beach.

*The hatch cover! Now it's just half the outrigger and the lines I've lost! Dad will be pleased! And if he's not? I'll deal with Dad if it happens.*

Christos jumped into the shore waves, dog-trotting along the beach to get the cover. Washing it in the tide, he slipped it over the for'ard hatch.

*Now we're ready to go.* He walked back to get the anchor, stopping beside the shark as he returned, reluctant to leave.

*They'll never believe me. They'll say you weren't that big. That I caught the reef and that's what broke the outrigger, lost the lines and ripped out the cleats.* Christos shook his head, then stopped, as though deciding something. He buried the anchor in the sand again and waded back out to *Li'l Bit*'s stern.

*I won't let them believe their lies. Not because I want to show off, like I did when I wanted to show them all the size of my fish, but because I want them to know the truth. I'll prove to them that what I say*

*I've done is what I've really done. That I looked you in the eye and thought I'd die. That I was frightened in parts of me I never knew existed. I'll prove to them that I needed help and Karis helped me, like there's always someone to help even in the darkest night of the soul. I'll prove to them that I am who I am and what I am is enough. I owe you that much because you died to set me free.* The thought hit him like a revelation. The thing he feared most had set him free. If the shark hadn't dragged them from the coral, *Li'l Bit* would have sunk. Christos fell to his knees in the water beside its head.

'We'll prove it!' he said, plunging the point of the filleting knife deep into its upper lip. 'You and me, brother.' It was hard work hacking and sawing, especially around the hinged joints. Christos was sweating when he stood again. In his hand he grasped the shark's massive gap-toothed jaws. He wiped the sweat from his face. Blood dripped from the wound on his hand.

'You won't be needing these now,' he said, wiping his blood onto the shark's snout, anointing it.

*Sorry. I never meant to catch you. I never wanted you to die. I only ever wanted one thing – to live.*

Then Christos, the fisherman, placed the shark's jaws into the kill-pit and stowed the anchor. Rinsing his hands, he shoved *Li'l Bit's* bow to sea, then climbed aboard to start the motor. He kicked her into gear and the dory idled forward, bouncing in the shallow water.

He thought about Karis – but now everything had changed. Now he was a year older and he knew who he would live for.

*Let dying take care of itself.*

They left the beach then, journeying out into the clear bay, away from the gold-veined, broken coral, until the grey fog swallowed them whole, until all that could be heard was the putt-putting of the exhaust. As the sun from darkness was rising, they headed home.

# ACKNOWLEDGEMENTS

With thanks to Carl Svendsen, Lyndie Malan, Viller Svendsen and Councillor Emeritus Mike Prior for their invaluable advice on mackerel dories and fishing. Thanks to Jack Stevenson for his memoirs of mackerel fishing, especially for some of the more colourful fishing expressions. Thanks to Steve Little for lending me the name of his old boat and to the fisher-tribe of Central Queensland for the liberties with fact I've taken in telling this tale. I never let the truth get in the way of a good story! Also thanks to Helen Chamberlin, Thyri Svendsen, Mark Avery, Laurel Jackman, Gay Girle, Robyn Kerr, Glen Svendsen, Robyn Sheahan-Bright, Shan Boller and the kids in her Book Club and Anne Svendsen for their comments on drafts and their enthusiasm. Thanks to Allan McDermott of Townsville Slipway Boatsales who helped with photos of a plywood dory. There are very few left.

Finally, thank you so much Leonie Tyle, publisher at Woolshed Press, for your faith, dedication and determination. Go, you good thing!

186

## A note from the author

I found inspiration for writing *To Die For* in many places. As a teenager I had access to a mackerel dory and spent many weekends fishing. Actually, it was less fishing and more mucking about in a beautifully responsive boat. Being out on the water on a perfect day always heightened my sense of freedom and of the beauty in the world. I tried to put into the novel some of this sense of awe at the beauty of being caught alive between the sea and the sky.

Being out on the dory was always a solitary activity for me, which, as a loner by personality, I very much enjoyed. This type of boat is designed for only one person to work from at a time. Everything about the dory is designed to make her both very seaworthy and a perfect fish-killing machine. Seen in that light, a dory and a shark have a great deal in common – both are ultimate predators and both are graceful but blunt about their business.

It was about this time, too, that I first read *The Old Man and the Sea* by Ernest Hemingway. Because I also went fishing a lot I really connected with the main character in that book. It is always a triumph to catch a fish, but there is also always a note of sadness when your worthy adversary dies. I hope I've managed to catch this feeling between Christos and the shark.

I was also inspired by the emotion I first felt when, as a kid in primary school, I heard my teacher read a story from an old local newspaper. The story described how a small sailing skiff had capsized in a storm in Keppel Bay only a few nautical miles from where I lived.

The boat had on board two men, a boy and a dog. As the boat was swamped and wouldn't support them all, the men tied the boy to the mast then swam off towards the nearest island. The boy was alone in the boat overnight and was found safe and well on the beach in Emu Park the next morning. I felt for him. What a night that must have been – alone, unable to move and in utter darkness. But it was worse for those left in the water. First the dog, then one man was taken by a shark. How must the last man left alive have felt as he struggled on through the storm towards the beach?

I've tried to use some of those feelings to infuse *To Die For* with a sense of what it may feel like to be alone in the darkness at sea and the courage it takes to keep swimming no matter what.

## Tiger sharks: the garbage guts of the ocean

- Tiger sharks grow to over 6 metres long and they can weigh over 500 kilograms. They live for up to 50 years.

- They will eat almost anything, from stingrays to dugongs, from sea snakes and turtles to . . . humans.

- Tiger sharks live in tropical and sub-tropical oceans around the world.

- The stripes that give tiger sharks their name are darker in younger sharks, but they grow fainter as the shark grows.

- Tiger sharks are considered very dangerous to humans, especially as they sometimes come into shallow water to find prey. But they aren't the most dangerous shark – the great white shark has more recorded attacks on humans.

VINTAGE CLASSICS

# Adventure galore

If you enjoyed *To Die For*, here are some more books full of adventure, bravery and survival against the odds. These books are also available as Vintage Classics.

### *The Old Man and the Sea* by Ernest Hemingway

Highly recommended by *To Die For* author Mark Svendsen, Hemingway's magnificent fable set in the Gulf Stream off the coast of Havana is the tale of an old man, a young boy and a giant fish. This story of heroic endeavour stands as a unique and timeless vision of the beauty and grief of man's challenge to the elements.

### *The Adventures of Huckleberry Finn* by Mark Twain

After a daring escape from a locked cabin, Huckleberry Finn takes off down the Mississippi River on a raft with a runaway slave called Jim. But plenty of dangers wait for them along the river – will they survive and win their freedom?

### *Treasure Island* by R.L. Stevenson

When young Jim Hawkins discovers a map showing the way to Captain Flint's treasure, he and Squire Trelawney set sail on the *Hispaniola* to search for the gold. Little do they know that among their crew is the dastardly pirate Long John Silver. Silver has a devious plan to keep the gold all to himself. Can brave Jim outwit the most infamous pirate ever to sail the high seas? Will he escape from Treasure Island alive?

***Swallows and Amazons* by Arthur Ransome**
The Walker children set sail on the *Swallow* and
head for Wild Cat Island. There they camp under
open skies, swim in clear water and go fishing for
their dinner. But their days are disturbed by the
Blackett sisters, the fierce *Amazon* pirates. The
Swallows and Amazons decide to battle it out, and
so begins a summer of unforgettable discoveries
and incredible adventures.

***The Jungle Book* by Rudyard Kipling**
When Father Wolf and Mother Wolf find a man-cub
in the jungle, they anger the greedy tiger Shere
Khan by refusing to surrender it to his jaws, and
rear the child as their own. But when little Mowgli
grows up, the pack can no longer defend him. He
must learn the secret of fire, and with the help of his
friends Bagheera the panther and Baloo the bear,
he faces his nemesis at last.

VINTAGE CLASSICS

# What is a dory?

Mackerel dories were small vessels (16 feet or just under 5 metres), common in the 1950s, 60s and 70s on the mackerel fishing grounds up the length of the Queensland coast. Made of plywood, they had small inboard motors. They were beautifully balanced boats designed to be towed by a larger 'mothership' out from coastal harbours to the reefs and shoals of the Great Barrier Reef. Being small, they used little fuel and enabled a fisherman to 'troll' (tow a lure or bait on fishing lines behind the moving dory) around the shoals and reef edges to catch mackerel and other reef fish. Several dories could operate simultaneously from one mothership. Dories are now very rare due to the advent of aluminium dinghies with outboard motors but … the name has been preserved by being passed on to these newer dinghies.

On the next page you can find a diagram showing the main parts of a mackerel dory.

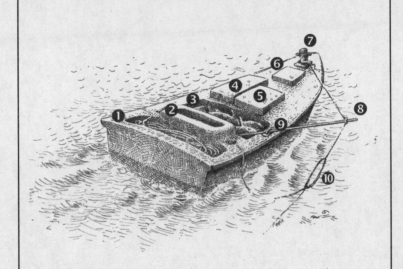

1. line tray
2. standing pit
3. kill pit
4. icebox
5. engine hatch
6. for'ard hatch
7. Samson post
8. outrigger
9. cleat
10. shockie